SCENT
OF
DESIRE

SHANEN RICCI

Cover designer: Stefanie Saw
Editor: One Love Editing
Proofreader: All Encompassing Books
Formatter: Stacey Blake

ISBN: 979-10-976027-3-4

Playlist

"Darkside" Grandson

"Devil Like You" Gareth Dunlop

"Sold My Soul" Caleb Mills

"Can't escape" Yawdel feat. Laurent John

"Storm" Ruelle

"I fell in love with the devil" Avril Lavigne

"My demons" Starset

"Eye of the Storm" Ryan Stevenson

"Burn" Edda Hayes & 2WEI

"Bad Romance" Lady Gaga

"I can't help falling in love with you" Elvis Presley

"Hurts Like Hell" Fleurie

"My Love Will Never Die" Claire Wyndham

Prologue

His name is the Devil's.

Born as a diamond in the rough,

The wrath of the ruler of hell is deadly.

King of darkness, he wears the invisible crown
of the souls he collects.

His name is the Devil's.

He trapped his queen with his infernal arms.

She planted a scent of hope into his cold realm,

With the promise that light will flower in the starless pit.

His name is the Devil's.

And to every Devil,

there is one weakness.

Chapter 1

Radcliff

Twenty years ago

Drums played in syncopated rhythms, matching the beats of my heart.

Different shades of green from the tall exotic plants blocked the view ahead to the lianas inside the jungle. It was too humid as Mom and I sank deeper into the wilderness, following our guide. The sound of the drums was getting closer, like a lion chasing after you before it devoured you until only your bones remained as an offering to the vultures.

I gazed at the ground, looking for the remains of victims from the past, but sand was itching my eye, clouding my vision. The sun was fading, but my flesh still burned. Light wasn't my friend.

Our guide, or Tiger's Eye as I named him, swept aside the savaged plants with his arm, clearing the way. A group of people who lived on the island was gathered around a fire. They either wore plaid outfits with diverse colored patterns or white tunics with some kind of white sheet on their heads. *Jewels.* My eyes sparkled at the sight. I had a thing for gemstones and associated my thoughts on people with them.

When our guide suggested we join them, my first instinct was to gaze upon my mother. I didn't like strangers, nor the souls of most people.

"Don't tell your father we're here." Mom's bright smile was enough to make me feel safe.

I nodded, and she intertwined our fingers together, leading us to the fire so we could take a seat. I didn't understand. People held machetes. A group of women waved smoking tree branches. I recognized the odor: it was sage. Mom used this for cleansing rituals. A priest drew secret symbols in the dust before he poured alcohol on top of it.

"They're honoring spirits," Mom whispered. She was a believer, just like the amethyst; she had pure wisdom and the gift of foresight. My mom could predict the future with a set of tarot cards—but she hid it from Father. He said it was witchcraft. I thought it was magic.

My eyes widened when I caught a glimpse of what was hiding beyond the smoke of the fire. Immense flowers stood like columns. They were taller than me in a purple color, with almandine garnet layers. Shivers traveled over my skin. I must be in a land of giants. A parallel universe.

I'd heard Father say earlier that this island had been corrupted, that we were there on a humanitarian mission to close a mine. That's why this morning, I'd searched for precious stones near the beach. I thought it'd help him. I heard diamonds were shining through the sunlight; that's why I wanted to hold one. But all I had found was a sunburn.

I wrinkled my nose. The flowers smelled weird, like they were from the ashes of an old fire. I felt like death filled my nostrils. It was creepy but not unappealing. An older woman shook a rattle and bell, ambling in our direction. She wore a white tunic that contrasted with the brown of her skin. She squatted in front of Mom, a light smile on her face.

"You seek freedom? Heal your sorrow?" the woman asked my mother, but the pitch of her voice meant she already knew the answer. Her gaze drifted to mine. "Is it your son?"

"My Radcliff, *mambo. Can the Loa* protect him?" Mom said with worry.

The mambo's lips curved into a half-smile. She approached closer, her hand reaching for mine. I pulled away, not used to strangers touching me. My eyebrows knitted together in hostility. I didn't like it. *She thinks she can read me.* My fist clenched.

"Protection isn't what the boy needs." She chuckled, and I swore something sparkled inside her eyes. "That boy. Strong. Like iron."

"What is it, then?"

"Let's find out," the woman added.

The mambo priestess headed to the center of the ceremony. Her eyes didn't leave mine, and I gulped. It looked like she wanted to penetrate my soul—even if Father was convinced mine was gone. I furrowed my brows harder and squinted my eyes. Offense was the best defense.

Drums beat harder. Hands clapped. Maracas shook. The mambo sang the same melody over and over again.

Limen balenn nan – o an n rele lwa yo.

Sonnen ason an – rele Papa Legba.

Nan kafou a, o nou angaje.

Papa Legba – louvri baryè pou lwa yo.

"They are invoking the spirits…" Mom murmured to me. "They're opening the gate between the world of the dead and ours."

The flames reverberated inside Mom's pupils, rising higher like they were possessed by a stronger force. The gate between worlds was truly opening. The dancers did aggressive warrior stances. Men seemed to slice and cut the thin invisible air with a sword. With their machetes, they were warriors. *Strong as iron. I'll be just like them when I grow up.* Their expressions were blank, focused on the task.

But it wasn't just men. Women followed with violent steps on the ground. They thrust their chests and lifted their legs high with each step. Most of them had paint that looked like flour on their faces. Sometimes, the dancers would jump or run frenetically. My heartbeat galloped as I watched them losing control of themselves.

My face switched constantly from shadow to light. The shadows on the red sand widened until they blanketed the huge flowers like demons rising above.

With the rising pulse of the beat of the drums, the dancers increased their movements. The mambo closed her eyes for an instant, stepping on the ground faster and faster like she wanted to break it. I felt the earth shatter under my feet. My heart followed the drums at a blistering pace. I put my hand on it, afraid it'd beat out of my chest.

But then, the mambo fell to the ground. The rhythm of the drums decreased. Everyone waited. Only the scared squawk of an animal echoed through the night. The mambo took a fistful of the sand before looking straight ahead of her. Her eyes were darker when she lifted herself up. Was she possessed by the spirit?

The music started again when the animal in question was brought out to the mambo. It was a chicken, which was struggling, beating its wings, its cries of horror piercing me from inside.

The mambo seized it by its legs as the animal fought for life. I gulped. Her gaze didn't leave mine. The fire rose higher. Steps hit the ground, again and again. Dancers spun in circles, singing all together in a language I didn't know.

Trance—this was what it was. I held my breath. I didn't close my eyes. Blood spread. The chicken was dead. The garnet blood tarnished the white outfit of the mambo. I curled my hand into a fist and dug it into the sand. I understood it was an offering. Some kind of sacrifice. I ignored the blood and erased the scream of the animal from my head.

The night owned the land, but their dancing didn't stop. I didn't move from my seat, but I felt my head spinning. I looked upon the flowers where the shadows of the dancers reflected. Then, the beats slowed.

The mambo walked to my mother and gave her a sign to stand up. "Erzuli tells you your suffering will end." She gestured to a man who arrived from behind her. He was holding a pot, which he brought to Mom. "That flower you shall cherish, and secrets you'll uncover. Look beyond what's in front of you. There is balance. What darkness owns, light shall remain."

"Thank you, mambo." My mom seemed touched when she accepted the pot into her hands. She did her thing when her smile was so big that her eyes twinkled and creased.

Both of them turned to me in synchronization. My pupils flared. My skin hissed. The mambo kneeled in front of me, her eyes like those of a wolf in the night. Different. Bigger. Her hand shook, and she tried to reach me once more. This time, I didn't flinch.

Her gaze went subtly white like a horror movie. It was creepy. Her eyes seemed to have rolled beyond her head. Her lashes fluttered hard as she looked heavenward. My heartbeat slammed in my throat.

"You. Your destiny." A tear fell down her cheek. "Linked to the Devil's corpse. *Papa Legba I*—"

She crouched on the floor. Her eyes squeezed shut. She seemed to be in a dull pain by the way she bowed her head down and gripped her stomach. Heavy seconds passed, and eventually, she stopped shaking. The spirit who had spoken to her probably vanished. My mom believed in prophecies. Me, I wasn't sure.

The mambo's eyes flickered to mine. They weren't white anymore. She tried to graze my cheek, but she retracted—she knew better.

"Love, boy. Love can deliver you," she murmured with the kind of smile a grandmother would give to her grandchild.

"What do you mean?" My mother rushed to my side, caressing my hair. I remained stoic. Maybe my father was right. I didn't have a soul.

"Great destiny, but shadows. So many shadows." The mambo covered her lips with her shaky fingers, her face wrinkling. "Pain. So much pain."

"Tell me what you saw!" my mother screamed.

"Hell," the woman deadpanned.

"What's all this?" *Oh no.* Father arrived through the plants and gunned his eyes at Mom and me.

We both stood up, and I stepped in front of Mom, squaring my shoulders. His eyes lit up in a threatening red color. His fists clenched. My father was taller than everyone else. He was the most imposing and scariest man I'd ever met.

"You brought *your* son into this satanic voodoo!" He stormed across the circle and pushed the mambo to the floor. My eyes widened, seeing the old lady hitting the ground brutally. Something stiffened my fingers, like a nerve flickering. No one did anything. They all waited. "You cursed him even more."

"He's your son too. The universe isn't black or white, darling. This isn't—" Mom squinted when Father grabbed her wrist. A painful expression appeared on her face, but she denied it by faking a smile in my direction. She did it again. Pretending that everything was fine while her soul was of the saddest gray color.

The mambo had her eyes fixed on my father with her lips twisted backward. My father grabbed me by the collar, and I had to struggle to keep my feet on the ground. He had an iron fist and was built like a mountain.

"Demon child. You'll have to be purified." He didn't even look at me before pushing me toward the plants to escape the ceremony. I clenched my fist, knowing a punishment would follow. It always did with him. "You want to cause my downfall, don't you?" he gritted out through his teeth.

I didn't reply, but a lopsided grin curved on my lips. I'd never had a chance to match my father's power. But tonight, I had found an emotion I could generate inside of him. *Anger.* I wished to never become my father. I wished to never have a weakness. To never feel anything so I wouldn't be broken—he wouldn't be able to break me.

Before disappearing through the brush, I flashed my eyes at the mambo once more. Her eyes glistened at me, another tear running down her cheek. The last thing she whispered to me was—

Devil.

And it got me wondering, which one was the bigger evil? My father or me?

Which one of us was the Devil?

Chapter 2

Lily

The Witch had made the aphrodisiac.

I gripped the corner of the desk, fighting the horde of thrills roaming my body. I took in all the air in the lab, but it wasn't enough. It felt like breathing in a hammam. My hand searched desperately for something to fight the effects of the aphrodisiac but overturned the vials, which shattered on the floor.

"Fuck," I dropped in a low whisper of pleasure.

My mouth parted, sucking in all the air as if it was the most succulent of all. The cloud of scent filled my nostrils and invaded each of my veins with its toxicity and magic. My cells mutated with carnal desire and hunger. Soon, my world would be consumed and reshaped by the aphrodisiac and its own vision.

"I—" The scents seemed to have shushed me, their invisible fingers on my lips.

Only one drop of the aphrodisiac had been enough to transport me into a midnight dream—the kind where the lovers would meet to consume their forbidden love and where great ideas would be gifted by an angel. It shook the boundaries of time and space, making the world around me slower.

It was a reverie of the senses that would exhibit my most hidden desires or even my worst impulses if I didn't end this now. The ones buried in the deepest place of my subconscious.

"To every light, there is its darkness," I breathed, unable to resist that spell. There was always a downside to something that powerful, and I was gonna get a taste of my own destructive creation.

The aphrodisiac was a weapon. It fed the dangerous desires that you didn't know slept inside of you. Monstrous ones that craved murderous and lascivious sins. The kind that if they were to erode and break through the day, they would not return again in the darkness. It'd be chaos.

The darkest part of your soul would rule over you.

Inside mine, I had no idea what I'd found and—

It began. The cloud of scents took shape and danced in a waltz around me. A heat invaded me like a growing sun, and I threw my neck backward, caressing my neck. Even my skin was no longer smooth but scaly like a snake's to shield me from the outside world. I bit hard on my lower lip in a lame attempt at stopping my senses from multiplying.

My nose was drugged, every note intoxicating me in a fairyland that would make the real world only bland and gray. I felt my pulse in my neck and the buzzing of cells inside me. I saw the hair on my skin hauled up, my eyes zooming in on the little details. Even the colors were brighter, more rosy.

But then, my view blurred, reality melting with a delicious

illusion. The lab disappeared slowly to turn into an immense greenhouse. The walls became transparent windows, with green ornaments like the most regal of greenhouses. The garden of the manor became a starlit sky, perched on top of the clouds.

My grip on the desk loosened, and I lost my equilibrium watching the star show. My body pulled all of my energy to my sex, which made my legs collide, and I fell on the floor. I blinked, the vision of the laboratory fading from my mind. I surrendered to the illusion and finally closed my eyes, the scent lulling me into a bewitching sleep.

When I opened my eyes again, I was inside that greenhouse, my wrists and ankles tied up by ruthless vines. The thorns dug under my skin, keeping me locked under their embrace. Their grip tightened, lifting me up in the air so my feet wouldn't touch the ground anymore.

Looking at the view facing me, the greenhouse had no door or window. It formed a large arch that would give free passage to the angels as well as to the monsters. There was only an ivy alley with little blue wildflowers that formed a path leading to a throne. And around it, the deep void and chaos.

The moonlight was so big and so close. It illuminated the spines and the skulls on a throne in a gloomy blue light. A shadow appeared, half gargoyle, half statue, a dark smoke enclosing him.

"What's happe—" The vines commanded my arms to rise above my head and spread my legs.

My aching core and burning stomach took control of my mind. Was it so bad to submit to this illusion after all? *Would it be so bad to…*

The shadow took the shape of a man. He was in black trousers, shirtless, with a scarred godly body of an Olympian. The epitome of strength, his abs formed a deep V. Smoke escaped from his mouth, and there was no wondering who this man forged into the darkness was.

"Radcliff," I called out.

With one gesture of his hand, he directed the vines to bring me to him. Which they did, making me entirely at their mercy. I was at the edge of the void, still in heaven, but at any time, I would plummet to hell.

"So this is what you crave, little witch?" Radcliff's rough voice betrayed a flicker of amusement when his lips curved into a thin line.

The vines caressed my skin, growing to encircle me in their embrace through knots that Radcliff seemed to command. My hands were tied behind my back as the vines walked their way over my cleavage, skirting my breasts. They went around my belly twice before circling my hips. They finished their way through the center of my belly to bypass my sex.

"Are you up for a game?" His voice echoed in my ears, his whisper scouring each of my cells.

I gasped under the pressure of the knots tightening. My clit throbbed, and I let out a moan. I should struggle—this was all wrong, but that bliss… That bliss was magnificent. I needed *more*. I was thirsty, blinded to Radcliff's will, dominated by the vines, and under the aching torment to satisfy myself.

"That's not real…" I tried to fight over the illusion.

"That doesn't mean we can't play," Radcliff added, circling around me like a ringmaster. "I want you bare for me."

The vines tore my dress and underwear, each piece slipping into the air until no memory remained. Naked and entrapped by the vines, I couldn't move or fight against Radcliff's intense gaze that roamed every part of my offered body.

His fingers slid down my stomach, and I caught my breath. They went up to my breasts, sending goose bumps to my core. He teased my nipples with his forefingers, which hardened at his contact. I tried to struggle, but I was trapped. He leaned over my chest, and his hot breath on my nipples sent a wave of heat, making my sex clench.

"You want to play?" he asked again with a sinister confidence.

"Yes." I gave up, shutting my mind off.

I inched my breasts toward him so that his mouth closed on my nipple, and his tongue worked across it, making me moan. Each flick of his tongue was possessive and earth-shattering. It felt like pure euphoria when he took possession of my other breast with devotion before his hand slapped my butt cheek, hard and merciless.

He then retracted, leaving me flushed and wanting. With a gesture of his hand, new vines encircled my throat, and my legs spread wide. His hand traveled to my inner thighs, and I rolled my hips, hoping he'd touch my aching clit. But he didn't. He only teased.

"Sshh." He kissed the lobe of my ear before nibbling it. "You'll beg for it. Now say yes, and I'll punish you like the witch that you are."

"Yes," I dropped, desperate and burning.

He gave a light slap to my clit, making me gasp. He did it again, harder this time, and the mixture of pain and pleasure made my inner thighs shake and my mind go into delirium.

"Again, please." I bit my lower lip so hard to contain the tears of pleasure that rolled down my cheek. Each part of me begged to be touched, kissed, and adored. "I beg you."

"Look at you…" His fingers stroked my folds without entering, and wetness pooled between my legs in reply. "You're so fucking wet, my goddess."

He then licked his fingers with the taste of me but didn't indulge me. He took a seat on his throne, his gaze black with desire. "Do you still want to play?"

"Yes…" The Devil was used to being in control. He wouldn't let me go that easily, and I didn't want to.

Radcliff wore an invisible crown of power. His smile was

Machiavellian when he clicked his fingers. In response, the lianas' knots loosened to form again in other places. The lianas took possession of my ankles and circled my legs and then my elbows and wrists while keeping their grip between my breasts and my waist.

In a matter of seconds, I found myself suspended and kneeling in the air above Radcliff's throne. My chest was at his eye level, my back arched backward, and my throat offered to him due to the liana that had fisted my hair in a ponytail, craning my head back.

Radcliff lit a candle, watching the wax forming. "It's time to plummet to hell together. Now, the question is, do you want it hot or painless?"

"Hot."

"Close your eyes," he ordered.

I complied, and within seconds, I felt the hot wax from the candle trickle down my back. My eyebrows knitted together, and my lips parted. The smell was different. *Jasmine.* He poured yet another drop of wax, and I gasped. *Vanilla.* The wax hardened and—

I slammed my eyes wide open.

A drop of sweat traveled on my forehead, and the heat slowly disappeared. I was inside the lab again, one of my hands between my thighs and the other near another vial that had shattered on the ground. Next to me, there were the essential oils of jasmine and vanilla that had been spilled. *The new smells must have pulled me out of the effect of the aphrodisiac.*

I regained my consciousness and wondered if this dream was the illustration of a desire buried deep in my subconscious that the aphrodisiac was able to reveal or if Radcliff had fed a darker side of me. Either way, it wasn't a good omen. *If Radcliff were to smell it, how would it affect him?* It'd be a fate worse than the Pandora's box unleashed to the world.

I cleared my throat and readjusted the folds of my dress as if nothing had happened. The illusion had vanished, like a dream you struggle to remember. I held the desk and pressed myself against it to get up. I contemplated the mess I had made. Spilled vials and papers on the floor. Messy hair and crimson face.

My stare latched on to the aphrodisiac.

That purple-red demonic vial.

It didn't contain magic, or if it did, it was dark witchcraft that should have never seen the light of the moon.

"What have I done?"

I had created the most dangerous weapon. One that was against nature, and something told me I'd pay the price for it.

Chapter 3

Radcliff

Well, that was fucking new.

It had been forever since I had dreamed, especially about my wretched past—and I was fine without it. The nothingness and shadows were pleasant. Calming. Comforting. I buttoned the french onyx cufflinks of my black dress shirt that I wore like a snake shedding its old skin. Speaking of skin, parts of my body still burned as if I'd been through a hellfire. A sweet reminder of the scarred beast that I was hidden underneath the expensive clothes.

I wasn't born nor made for emotional connection and carnal needs. A ray of light and dust pierced through the opaque curtains, which didn't help me, blinding my sight. Just like Lily, it hurt. It was unfamiliar, destroying me slowly, invading itself into my unwelcoming realm.

The note she had left beside my bed was living proof of it. She had the handwriting of a teenager. Naive and optimistic. It was obviously scented, probably from one of her pink flowers.

A ghost of a smile appeared on my lips nonetheless. It quickly disappeared when the knocking on my door became incessant, its increasing tempo, like a bird pecking the wood, one of extreme annoyance. I was late. I had slept too long. And most importantly, I had a strong urge to roar to whomever that was and cut their throats off. At least, I was pleased to notice something about this morning was normal.

I wrenched the door open, loosening the old handle inside my palm, only to see Mrs. Walton's gaze widening before she took a step back, colliding with the wall of the hallway. She didn't speak, but she was too emotive to hide her loud thoughts. I edged a step back from the doorstep so she could enter, but she remained glued to the wall.

I dropped the broken handle to the floor. "We need a new handle."

She nodded, her hands gripping the wall behind her as if afraid of being embroiled in a frightening tornado or falling into a precipice. She would have more chances of survival with those fates compared to the irritation she was causing me right now.

Her eyes, obviously ignoring the sight of me, traveled and locked on the sheets on the floor. Sheets with traces of red blood. She swallowed, her face whitening like a ghost. *Great.* It was easy to see where her mind went.

"I didn't kill her." I didn't know why I justified myself. She would have known the moment Lily came back, pouring dirt everywhere with Cerba, laughing around the manor. Plus, I had many wicked things I craved to do to that witch, but death wasn't an outcome I'd allow her to have.

Mrs. Walton squinted her eyes in mistrust and carefully entered the "crime scene." For a moment, I thought of firing her. But then, I'd have to find a replacement. Someone neither judgmental nor talkative—a rather impossible mission. At least she already ticked a box on the talkative part.

The old shrew roamed the bedroom. It amused me for a beat, scrutinizing her on a quest for clues. She looked like a clairvoyant, searching for a sign of a spirit to whisper her tales of the past. She picked up the sheet, and her lips curled into a smile that quickly faded when she felt the weight of my stare upon her.

That morning was definitely not normal.

I sauntered to my balcony, wishing for the icy air to cool me down. It didn't work. The ruthless winter was pulling away to let the annoying blossoming spring rise. Birds sang, and the ghostly forest didn't seem so hostile.

In the midst of all those changes, the biggest of them all appeared across my garden. Near the cliff, that flower goddess was playing in the green field with that traitor Cerba.

Her laughter mingled with the singing of the birds. Cerba jumped around her, ignoring the fact that dogs can't fly. Lily wore some kind of dusty rose/camel corset dress with pleats all over. Her tousled hair, worn in long, messy curls, was tempted to be hung up by the brooch I offered her. She looked like madness in its beauty. A radiating heat traveled to the pulse between my legs.

It didn't help when she spun in circles, her dress swaying with the wind. I had a view of her white lace panties from all angles. It needed to be ripped apart. I would fuck her on that field she loved, slamming deep inside her as she dug out the flower roots, trying to hold on. It'd be a merciless mess. I'd even consider tying her against a tree, naked and at my mercy. The cold air would harden her nipples, and I'd shut her up with those panties of hers.

I was hard and frustrated.

I tried to regain some semblance of control when Lily lay in the middle of the daisies like an angel. She savored the sun warming her skin. She was where she belonged. Truth was, I had never noticed the grass on my property could grow flowers—apart from the greenhouse. Only weeds were growing, but Mr. Walton tore them off immediately. It was always dry and dead. Until her.

My thumb traced my mouth as I leaned on the railing. I zoomed my stare to her, heartbeat rising. Her cheeks were getting pink under the sun, her lips curving upward. My Adam's apple bobbed at the realization, acid irritating my throat.

I'd never let her go.

Not even after the first day of spring.

I'd make another contract if I had to.

The word "mine" appeared in the form of a lullaby haunting my mind. The Devil inside of me was laughing abundantly. I was his puppet.

I brought a cigar between my lips and lit it up. The greasy off-white smoke undulated across the air, tarnishing the colorful scenery. I disliked smoking. I only indulged in it to have more patience during social events. The pungent coal was a way to calm my nerves—or today, my frustration.

I took out my phone, calling Hugo. Yesterday, I had made a decision I was firmly set on. It wasn't rational, but chaos was calling me on.

"Rad, what's up?" Hugo was out of breath. This fucker was either fucking or running his lungs out.

I exhaled the acrid black smoke, a sardonic hint of a smile on my face. "I have a surprise for a special someone I want you to deliver."

"The tone of your voice tells me otherwise." I had to admit, Hugo had learned to get to know me over the years. "Not that I'm not liking the sound of that. Who's the lucky person?"

I scratched the cigar inside my palm, breaking it down into ashes. "Carmin. He touched Lily at the club."

If you crossed the Devil, you'd have to pay the price. Every action has consequences. Especially the ones including what belonged to me. I wasn't one to share, and I certainly wasn't clement with people thinking they could break my rules.

"That's what it's all about." He paused. "I thought you didn't do personal revenge."

"It's not. Just a message." A kind reminder of what my wrath could be. "Plan a meeting with his investors. I'm sure there are some parts of Carmin's on the buyout," I implied.

Hugo chortled. "Anything else?"

"Never do something behind my back ever again."

I hung up. I knew he was the one who'd brought her to the club that night. The memory of her dancing in front of all those bastards and their perverted thoughts made me want to squash their pitiful skulls.

Hugo was just like Mrs. Walton in a way. Both had the talent to meddle in my personal business. A thing they'd never done before Lily.

She was still lying on the grass, Cerba watching over her. She was peaceful, and yet she had no idea all the destruction I'd do to protect her. She had given me back a piece of my heart.

But hell, it was the worst one.

I'd do anything for her.

Especially the cruel, the damned, and the worst.

Chapter 4

Lily

The warmth of the sunlight hugged me with its golden arms. It kissed my face, beaming down on me with brilliant rays, and I had to close my eyes. My fingertips grazed the grass, the birds rocking me in a heavenly melody. I lay in the midst of the daisies and poppies, a fresh swell of wind bringing to my nostrils the smells of the upcoming spring.

It was earthy and aqueous, the scent of wet grass and green scents symbolizing the blossoming new. I wished to be transported to Paris for an instant. I missed sauntering by the alleys of cherry blossom trees and the flower shops full of roses.

Spring was my favorite season.

But spring this year had a different meaning for me. An uncertain outcome.

The sunshine had left my face, replaced by an imposing shadow. I thought it was a dark cloud until Cerba wiggled her tail on my dress. Someone had masked the sun, matching its brightness with his somberness. Only one person had this godly power.

My eyelids peeled open. My heartbeat increased at the sight of Radcliff standing up tall and menacing on top of me. He had a cold-blooded grace, one that could bring the envious and prestigious kings out of their graves. The sun tried to pierce from behind him with narrowing rays contrasting with another of his pitch-black suits.

My lips curved into a smile, and the merciless view of him brightened my conflicted heart. He was a dark angel that had come to capture me. A chill of fear coursed through my core at the thought of telling him I had made the aphrodisiac. Would he use it as a destructive means and become only a dark spirit thirsty for revenge? Would he get rid of me and his heart once he had what he wished for the most? Nothing would ever be the same.

"Lily." The rasp of Radcliff's voice tingled my insides. "Back in your element."

He eyed the flowers encircling me almost with disdain, as if they were the wicked hands of men groping me.

"Why don't you join me?" My teeth tugged at my bottom lip.

One of his eyebrows rose so slightly it was almost imperceptible. It felt like I had asked him to play some childish game, and he stepped away, letting the sun blind me. Handling the heat of the sun was one thing, but the one he ignited inside of me was tremendously warmer.

"Perhaps I prefer to look at you from where I'm standing."

I held the chaos in his eyes. His irises didn't let in any light like a stormy cloud. It was a house where purple shadows would try to evade, a mystery wedging into the depths. A tale as old as time.

21

"That's why you came here? To look at me?" I sat up and passed my fingers through the flowers stuck in my hair, which I tied into a side braid. Then, like barrettes, I pricked the daisies back into my hair to embellish it.

"I warned you, you will not escape me."

"What if I try?"

"A little too late for that, little witch. I've fingered you. Tasted you. Been inside you." His eyes shimmered, a sly grin slanting his mouth.

My braid came undone at the end. A jolt of hot lust, like red camellias and roses, pooled between my legs by the threat and rawness of his tone.

"Hell, you've provoked me in every possible way. Every action has consequences," he added.

Those were consequences I'd gladly assumed and let them consume me whole. He was wrong, and there was no denying something magnetic and almost demonic united me to him. Us, it was not rational, nor a blessing from heaven.

By giving Radcliff what he and I craved, I'd fallen on the dark side, with the uncertainty to drive back to the light. If our obsessions had engendered the most unholy weapon, what would our desire give birth to?

"You didn't answer my question." My voice was demanding and weak.

"I'll burn the world to find you." He was deadly serious.

I thought we were playing around, but the seriousness of his tone sent a shiver down my spine. I believed him. He'd burn the world, and it aroused me. The way he radiated power, the impossible bowing to him. The way he cloaked the night, how his surrounding darkness could fight the light of day. The mysteries encircling him and the moonlit tale we could write.

"How would you find me then?" I continued the game, my bare feet stroking the daisies.

"I'd have mercy only on a short field of lilies of the valley. The only place you could possibly be. Easy enough." A cruel smile slipped free from his lips.

I let out a laugh. "I'm that predictable, am I?"

He didn't reply, but his stare crept under my skin, lingering over the length of my legs. My dress heaved with the wind that rebelled in a squall, and he seized this opportunity to glimpse at my panties. I held my dress down, leaning forward. This time, his gaze flickered to the valley between my breasts. With a simple glance that had the power to strip me naked, my heart missed a heartbeat. The flowers in my hair blew away in the midst of this tension.

"Inflicting chaos isn't something I'd want you to do," I blurted out, the swell bringing to my nostrils his tantalizing smell that nestled me in the comfort of his darkness.

"That's why I know you won't escape. You would never want to be responsible for that kind of fate." He paused. "You're *good*."

I gulped at the harsh way the word "good" escaped from his mouth. Good and bad. Hero and villain. Such black-and-white statements that were so close to each other. The roles could reverse so easily, and a heart could readily blacken.

"Perhaps I'm not that good," I murmured as Radcliff shifted back in my direction, his interest piqued. "You see my goodness, but you can't see yours."

"And which goodness would that be?"

"The way you're with me," I affirmed with certainty.

"That's not goodness. That's…" He searched for his words before a cunning line twisted his lips. "Possession."

"Is that what I am to you? Just a possession?" My heart galloped, fleeing from my chest.

Radcliff hid the sun from me again, a knot tightening his jaw. "You're mine, Lily. That was your decision."

"Because I want to." I knitted my brows together, exhaling all the breath I was holding. "Not because I'm a possession."

I drilled my eyes on him, refusing to be his pretty pet and an obsession he couldn't get rid of.

"What are you expecting from me exactly, Lily?" He gritted his teeth and cracked his knuckles. "Sweetness? Love? Because I cannot give you any of that."

Or you're just afraid to allow yourself to feel like I already made you feel. We had played a winter game, and he had won, but this one, the game of spring, I wouldn't allow him to win.

Because now, I knew his weakness.

Me.

"Respect. I'm an equal." My fingers dug into the earth, taking a handful to the point of uprooting the grass to keep my emotions in check. "Your equal."

Radcliff knelt in front of me, his scent rushing to my senses as I inhaled the delicious inferno that he was. In a threatening tone, he questioned, "Do you feel ready for this ordeal?"

I would be ready to stand by his side as long as he let me in.

My lips parted, but no sound came out. His fingers brushed my throat, feeling my pulse throb. Poker-faced, he gripped it, his blackness testing mine. He wanted me to be at his mercy, scared and uneasy, but I did not move. I let him crane my neck backward, tightening his grip on my throat.

Radcliff would never hurt me. He wasn't the villain of my story. His thumb then traveled to my lips, stroking their outline.

I parted them and took his thumb inside my mouth. I sucked it and dropped, "Yes."

Our eyes merged on common ground.

He didn't respond, but we both knew a new deal had been made.

"You don't want to join me?" I asked again.

"I should go." He cleared his throat, his gaze not leaving my mouth. The darkness of his pupils did not conceal the things he not so secretly craved to do to me.

"If you stay, I'll let you in on a secret." My voice was playful even though it wasn't a secret, truly. The aphrodisiac was ready; that was a fact.

A ghost of a smile stretched his lips before Radcliff rose up. "Flower goddess, I never follow up on blackmail."

As he'd have left at any second, I held him back by calling out, "I made the aphrodisiac."

His eyes flashed. His Adam's apple bobbed. His nostrils flared.

"It's not ready yet." For some reason, my heart hammered frantically. My instincts scolded me, whispering that this was all a bad idea, but I couldn't lie to him. "It needs a couple of weeks of maceration still. We'll have to wait, but I just wanted to let you know."

His gaze remained firm, and I thought he'd leave without a word. I had accomplished the impossible, and he showed no sign of enthusiasm.

He readjusted the cuffs of his suit, focused on the task. "Then you deserve a reward."

"W-what reward?"

"Meet me inside in a couple of hours. Mrs. Walton will deliver you a card."

My eyes widened. "A card?"

"Yes, to keep the mystery, my little witch."

On that note, he darted across me and went back to the gloominess of his manor as I watched him disappear inside like a ghost haunting the place. I let out a ragged breath and picked a daisy. I lay on my stomach on the grass and rolled the flower between my fingers, just like Radcliff used to do with his signature card.

Would I save Radcliff's soul?

I focused on the question and brushed over each petal of the daisy.

Yes. I pulled out a petal.

Certainly. Another.

It's too early to tell. Another.

Small chance. One more.

Never. Another.

I continued, my heart contracting each time I pulled out a petal. They were becoming fewer and fewer. *It's too early to tell.* Dread twisted in my guts. *Small chance.* I froze on the last remaining petal, feeling engulfed by a pain in my chest.

Never.

Chapter 5

Lily

Ghastly tendrils of fog blurred the view outside while ravens sang the melody of the damned. The gloomy trees and their greedy fingers of adoring acolytes tried to penetrate through the walls of the Devil's house.

I shut the window and folded the letter into my dress's pocket, along with the old metallic key Radcliff had sent me. The card he wrote me indicated: *"Follow the path of darkness, to sweep the door of pleasure open."* To that, he had added the directions to follow. It was rather more mystical than explicative, but so was he. How many secrets was he hiding?

I grabbed the old brass candlestick with a lit-up candle—a scented one with sage that would clean the evils from the place. As

I left my bedroom, the creak of the door filled the ghostly silence, and the heavy decaying air wafted up my nose.

The hallway was empty. It seemed endless with narrowing walls that would suffocate me as I passed through the paintings depicting the infernos. They glared at me to the point that I could hear their cries, their torture, the underworld calling me in a whisper.

The candle fluttered the moment I arrived at the child's painting, the one with the expression so dark and tragic, holding a particular beauty. His eyes landed on me each time, no matter where I stood. They had the power to stop my heart and freeze my cells. The hair behind my neck raised, my body speaking the emotions I couldn't quite describe nor remember. I wouldn't be surprised if the phantom of the child haunted this place.

I put a hand around the flame to keep the air from turning off the light, but it continued to fidget as if his ghostly spirit was trying to communicate. There was no draft, but the flame blew sideways, and smoke rose. A gasp escaped my lips. My shoulders tensed. A silent scream threatened to come out.

The flame rekindled, and my gaze fell on the haunted painting. Now, I was convinced this child had died in the most atrocious way. I paced to the last door with the heavy clamps, and with shaking hands, I slammed it open with the key.

"What's—" My breath caught, and I almost lost my balance in the rush.

Behind the door, there was only a stone staircase, which descended into the depths of the mansion. It looked like a spiraling tower, without any flicker of light.

"Okay, Lily, don't freak out." My footsteps echoed on the cold steps, like a stone falling into a deep well.

He did it on purpose.

Radcliff knew my fears and could read me with ease. If I conquered my demons and tamed them, he would reward me.

You take pleasure in being afraid, little witch.

I could hear the whisper of his voice replying to my soul.

Arriving at the end of this staircase, I then crossed a long corridor with stones that could have looked like skulls, as if the foundation of the manor was built on skeletons. A gloomy sign of wrath and death. The air was cold, with no draft passing under this secret passage, which felt like a walk inside the catacombs.

My grip tightened on my light, for fear the candle would blow out. A shiver ran through my spine, thinking it was the road to a sunless prison. I didn't feel safe being underground.

As I observed the dusty wood door marking the end of the tunnel, I heard the echo of burning ovens through the stones. The flames were crackling; somebody was adding charcoal below. It was like feeding a hungry steam train, and that was how I imagined the underworld to smell like—a firewood of sacred fire from which curls of smoke escaped in a dark fragrance. Suave, woody notes of cedar, sandalwood, and coffee beans.

Wrenching the door open, I faced an underground cave with the air of a hammam. Mist blurred the orange burning lights of the torches, like those found in castles, hanging on the walls. Two flaming stone columns stood at the end of the roman bath like a god's temple.

It was square with a ledge inside, a milk bath covered with black petals, which swirled in the creamy color. I had never seen a bath nor a place like this. It was a midnight Arabian dream.

The petals were from the *Queen of the Night* tulip, her sweet and floral odor filling my nostrils. Knowing Radcliff, he didn't leave any details to chance. It was a coronation.

People are baptized in holy water.

And this was my baptism inside the Devil's lair.

Steam escaped from the bath, the ovens below the stones probably heating it. Across the fog, by the columns, enthroned on a royal chair, was Radcliff. Like a regal king, in a black velvet towel wrapped around his hips, his presence stopped my heart. The torchlight illuminated only part of his face; as usual, he remained in the shadows. His powerful muscles melted me. His imposing biceps glowed in a golden sunset tone as drops of sweat slid through his defined abs and deep V.

"Radcliff," I dropped, already burning hot.

He did not get up, his obsidian stare scorching me more than the heat of the room. And then, he ordered, "Strip."

I blinked and glanced at my dress, about to contest him. But instead, I shut my mouth and held his gaze that couldn't be refused. He ran his hand over his jaw, analyzing me, his mind commanding me by reading into mine. I obeyed his order and sensually pulled the zipper of my dress down. I lowered my shoulder straps and let my dress fall on the cobblestones.

I swallowed, thinking he was done with me, and I inched closer to meet him, my skin made golden by the flames.

He leaned in, his eyes sparkling with mischief. "Strip. Everything."

I unclasped my bra, which met the floor next to my dress, alongside my panties, which followed right after. Naked in front of him, I let his gaze strip me even more than I was. It lingered on me as if I was a creation meant to be adored, belonging to him in a contract made of the ink of life.

"Pull your hair to your back. I want to see you."

I didn't resist and let my hair caress my back. I tugged a strand of it behind my ear, nibbling my lower lip. His stare stopped on my breasts, tracing every curve, devouring them with his eyes, and my nipples hardened in response. He then lowered his gaze to my waist and hips until he reached my sex. He clenched his jaw, holding in all of his darkest cravings, his demons feasting on the view. The way he reacted strongly to me made my hair raise and my knees buckle.

His silence was torture. My mouth parted, and my body tingled, needing more than a phantom touch. I needed him to submit to his devastating desire.

The corner of his lips quirked up, appreciating the effect he was having on me.

"Enter the bath, flower goddess," he tempted me.

Magnetized, I ambled slowly toward the bath, my steps led by the butterflies inside my belly. My eyes didn't move away from his. The milk hugged my feet, and the feel of it could rock me in the sweetest of melodies.

Covered up to my upper legs, I stopped and collected the milk in the hollow of my hands. A teasing smile appeared on my lips, and I let the white liquid fall on my breasts, passing by my nipple until it reached my stomach. His eyes followed when, with a finger, I traced the path of the liquid, caressing myself leisurely.

Radcliff tightened his grip on the throne before he brought his fist to his mouth and bit one of his fingers to contain his impulses.

I engulfed myself inside the bath up to my neck. I swept my arms in the liquid, leaving it staining my skin porcelain white. I tilted my head back, and the black petals caught in my wet hair, forming a dark crown.

"You're not fully wet." Radcliff leaned forward, and the flames next to him mirrored his demons, rising higher. His eyes contrasted with the red, the irises as black as his pupils.

I dove under the milk. It was like being inside a soft cloud, a heavenly dream you don't want to wake up from. Coming out, I blinked away the white liquid before I sat down on the ledge and outstretched my arms on either side. My breasts broke through the surface as drops of milk ran down my forehead to my lips. I caught one with my tongue and licked it.

"There is room for more than one person inside this bath." I wanted to enchant him, spellbind him like the siren he wanted to trap.

"If I come, I'll ravage you," he threatened in a tone that entailed scorching debauchery and wicked paradise.

"And that's not what you want?" I gulped, the tropical heat of the smoke drying my throat.

"I want more than that, little witch." He removed the knot from his towel and let it fall to the side, freeing his hard manhood in front of me. "Spread your legs."

My hands clutched the ledge harder behind me. I parted my legs wildly, a tenor echoing between my thighs.

"Touch yourself." His hand slid on his hardness, stroking himself at the sight of me. His movements were fluid and slow, yet all of his muscles were tense. The veins of his arms stood out in a purple color like an up-to-no-good potion spreading. "Touch yourself as if you'd die if you don't. Submit to your pleasure. I want to hear you cry out from those precious lips of yours."

My cheeks turned crimson, and then, the shyness slipped away under his empowering words. I lowered my hand between my crotch and arched my back, my breath cutting short in slow, ragged intakes. I reached the part of me where only he had touched me and caressed myself shamelessly, my eyes locked on his masculine hand pleasuring himself.

The milk lapped across my skin under the pace of my rolling hips. I was aroused by the way he ate me with his stare. How he envied the way my fingers touched my clit. How it tortured him to see my naked breasts bouncing without being touched. The way he groaned, thrusting his manhood inside his palms.

"Roll your nipple between your forefingers, and as you do, imagine I'm sucking and flipping it." His voice echoed like multiple shadows across the room.

I closed my eyelids, caressing my breast. My head fell backward, my throat offered for his invisible kisses. The heat transported me to a humid jungle where I was the slave under the torture of a king. Desire was mortal. A need.

I rolled my nipple with my fingers and moaned. I heard the stroking of his cock. It was fast. His grunts. It was like he was chasing after me, and if only he would catch me, he would do to me all manner of unholy sins.

"Now tug it and give it a slap because you've been bad teasing me like that."

I tugged on my nipple, my other hand taking a handful of my breast, imagining it was his touch worshipping me. I punished myself and slapped my pink nipple. My back arched in response, feeling the delicious ecstasy of pain melting with pleasure. I tugged on my other, my lips parting for a loud moan to slip free.

"Beautiful, flower goddess," he grunted, a rasp in his voice. "My tongue is now on your clit, my head buried between your legs."

"Yes," I dropped in desperation, under the spell of his voice. Instantly, I pressed my thumb on my clit and rolled circles around it. My body contracted, butterflies blooming in my stomach.

"Now, ride me, Lily."

Still with my eyes closed, I pressed harder, stretching my legs as far as I could on either side of the bath. I lifted my pelvis to feel more friction, feeling the bolt of pleasure building up.

"That's it. You're riding me. Faster."

His voice penetrated each of my cells. I quickened my pace, my fingers going numb. The milk lapped above my mouth. I could drown, but I didn't care. My body clenched under the firebolts of lust, and I snapped my eyes open.

"Don't!" he roared.

I snapped them shut again. "I want to see you."

"If you misbehave, you won't come. Follow the rules, flower goddess." I heard footsteps. Was he coming my way?

I nodded, not stopping my frantic pace, the heat taking my breath away.

"I flick one of your nipples as I'm fisting your hair. I devour you. Ride me, Lily."

Yes. My hips rolled, my legs shaking, the illusion of me riding his face continuing. My orgasm arrived like an unpredictable tornado that would shatter everything on its way. It burst into me, my clit pulsing like a mad heart.

"Oh my god!" I cried out, the last touch on my clit sending me to heaven.

"Not god," he whispered. "The Devil."

I took a short intake of breath and opened my eyes slowly. The view ahead of me was blurry, but I could see that Radcliff wasn't on the throne anymore. A breeze caressed my neck, and I spun around.

Radcliff appeared from behind me. He was sitting on the edge of the bath, displaying his iron strength with glowing muscles and wrapping up the room with his imposing aura. His scar tissues from old wounds displayed small breaks in the shape of cuts and slices with the heat, making his flesh shine. In one of his hands, he held a fruit of the brightest red.

Pomegranate.

With a knife, he cut it in half, then in a quarter so I could see the juicy dark burgundy seeds inside. He tilted a part of the fruit toward me like an offering.

"Your lips," I murmured. "They taste just like that."

"Perhaps because it's the fruit of the dead. It belongs to hell." He edged closer to me, and I craned my neck to meet his gaze and the strands of his raven hair dropping on his forehead. "Legends say if you eat some seeds, you'll be bound to the person who fed them to you. It would grant immortal life, apparently."

It was the forbidden fruit. "Is that supposed to scare me?"

His lips turned cruel. "That depends if you believe."

My heart hammered as Radcliff towered dangerously closer to me. Our breaths connected, my nostrils getting drawn to the exotic ruby-rich aroma of the juices and the winey and sweet aroma of the seeds. All of that wrapped inside Radcliff's dark fragrance to transport me inside a horse-drawn carriage passing through the middle of a maleficent enchanted forest.

"Care to have a bite?" the Devil tempted me.

I parted my lips as a reply. He brought the fruit above my mouth and squeezed it. I let the juice fall on my lips like the most delicious nectar. I drank each drop at the price of being bound to hell. It created some kind of trance in me. He fed me like I was his Cleopatra. I bit the seeds and licked my lips, not wanting to waste a drop.

But the red liquid had fallen from my lips to travel over my breast. Radcliff stopped the course of the juice when it reached my nipple. His fingers traced teasing circles, skimming on my bare skin with adoration. The juice tinted part of my body in a poppy color—the flower of offering to the dead.

Another drop of pomegranate juice fell on the creamy dream of the milk bath. Like a bloodstain, it diffused into the whiteness.

It was a simple act. Yet, I knew the consequences would be fatal.

"What now?" I dared to tease.

"You're mine."

He entered the tub like a warrior of the night or a demon prince reaching the forbidden heaven. The milk hugged his darkness, and the red blood elixir of the remaining pomegranates spread inside the bath like unholy water.

Radcliff positioned himself behind me. His breath tingled my neck, and the flames inside the room shook as if a violent draft had threatened to shut them off. Shivers spread, and he fisted my hair in a ponytail. His lips kissed my neck, finding all the sensitive spots that made my head fall backward.

Hunger poured inside my heart, and I arched my back for my

butt cheeks to tease his hardness. I sought to touch him, my hand traveling to his manhood. Just as I did, taking him inside my milky palm, he cuffed my hand behind my back, keeping control of the situation.

"Oh, little witch, you shouldn't have done that," he breathed, half with a wicked laugh, half grunting. "It wasn't supposed to go like that."

The word "why" was on the tip of my tongue when his hardness brushed over my folds. It diffused into a loud moan when he slammed into me, igniting my world in a red-tinted movie. At first, a shout of pain pierced through my core, and then, the line blurred with pleasure. His drives were forceful, his grip on my hips hard, as if he had no control over his demonic compulsions and was afraid of letting me go.

I dug my nails into his hands, searching for something to hold, feeling him deeper than he'd ever gone before. Our exchange smelled of a volcano erupting into a red sky, where poppies grew like giants and beauty was built on chaos.

"Radcliff…" I moaned.

That's when he gripped my throat to bring my back to his torso and sealed his lips on mine. I kissed him with all my strength and soul, and neither of us pulled away for fear it'd be the last, that we were going to be torn from each other. His tongue invaded my mouth to meet my own, and I let him consume me.

Our kiss was beautiful, in the way pain was. The simmer of our darkness was building up, until the searing fire aroused us to a point of no return. Blood flowed in my veins with adrenaline, and the stirring pain made my heart gallop.

It was also magical and haunted. A total abandonment. In each of his thrusts, he created another world for us. An illusion. A magical realm where we were rulers.

His calloused hand clutched my breast as his other slapped my butt cheek. My sighs of pleasure echoed across the room, engraving themselves into the stones forever. Radcliff's tall shadow shook on the walls, growing larger. The hardness of his grip on my butt cheek made me shift my eyes to him.

He may have pounded hard into me, dominating me with all his dark aura, but his eyes were solely mine. I saw the agony and conflict inside of them. I had the power over him: the one that made him feel. I traced with my gaze each of his muscles as they contracted. He tugged my hair, and a gasp escaped my mouth.

"Lily," he groaned.

He released his hold on me and made me bend over, cuffing my wrists with one of his hands. The other gave another slap on my butt cheek, and the tips of my breasts touched the milky bath. It wasn't so white anymore. Purple and crimson shadows colored it with the image of my flaming pleasure.

I rolled my hips to meet his merciless drives and lifted my head to not crumble inside the bath. My knees buckled, my eyes rolling behind. I bit my lower lip so hard that I tasted the metallic tang of blood.

I let myself be carried away by the moment. The steam of the bath and the heat inside me made me boil. My cheek grazed the milk in total abandonment, and then my head was under, plunging into the bath. I held my breath, letting the soft feel of milk permeate my face.

Radcliff brought my head out of the bath, making me spin around so fast that my senses abandoned themselves to his. We faced each other, and his lips nibbled on my neck as if his craving couldn't be satiated. He lifted me with ease, and the drops ran down my skin.

I wrapped my legs around his hips, and my fingers tangled in his hair. His pace increased harder and deeper. My breath cut off, suffocating. His grunts grew animal and primal. My eyebrows knit together as the waves of pleasure slammed into me, my clit pulsing with need. I dug my nails into his skin, and he gripped my leg in a way that would leave a bruise for days.

His final thrust sent me to hell.

Separately, we were black and white, a world without color with two extreme scents.

Together, we formed a red-tinted one, a magical potion of scents.

My vision clouded with small stars like glitters. I didn't trust my legs to support me, and when Radcliff put me down, I'd have tripped down the bath if it wasn't for his arm hooked around me, holding me protectively. I buried my head in the hollow of his right neck, and he pulled me in his embrace.

"You caught me." A soft smile slipped free.

"I will, always." His tantalizing hot breath brushed on the left side of my nape, and in a murmur, he added, "Just like you'll always hear my whisper on your left shoulder."

"Is that a threat?"

"No, it's a promise."

"It's romantic in a way," I mused, knowing that it meant his spirit would always be by my side.

"Having the Devil's voice haunting you like a ghost isn't something one would have described as romantic."

So, we'll just have to write a romance of our own.

One born of the madness in our hearts and the obsession of our souls.

Chapter 6

Lily

Creating the perfect bouquet was like doing the most detailed personality test.

You had to take into account the physical aspect, then the size, the meaning, and finally, the smell.

Lying on the grass, I picked the narcissus flowers in the field. They grew by the cliffs, facing the devastating wind and unable to escape the most violent of vicissitudes. Narcissus, the flower that held the significance of joy and, at the same time, death. I rose up from the ground and brought her to my nostrils, smelling her heady and opulent, floral yet animalic scent. It was similar to a hyacinth in a way.

I added the narcissus to the poppies I carried in my arms. They were the color of passion and blood, with notes of vanilla and cherry blossoms. I completed my bouquet with a firewitch, the flower that could resist any type of heat. A divine flower sent directly from the gods. Purple calla lilies for a touch of darkness. And to finish, the passionflower, a sensual smell coming from another time and place.

My bouquet was a rainbow of colors and scents, yet it was for the tenebrous Radcliff.

I took the black ribbon from my pocket and tied a knot between the stems of the flowers. A butterfly landed there, finding comfort. I chuckled, holding out my finger so the butterfly would fly toward it.

"Spring is blossoming, cutie. Where are your friends?"

The butterfly, as he or she understood me, flew from my finger to rest on my bouquet, clapping her wings.

Flowers were her friends too.

"Yeah, me too." I stroked a petal, remembering when I used to organize funerals each time Mom cut a flower.

I had my own cemetery, and each of them had their own name. Until one day, my mom told me it was okay to pick flowers—if you did it right. She said you have to cut a flower in such a way she'd grow back even more magnificent. Since that day, I abandoned the graves, and I grew with the certainty that I could immortalize a flower in time with a scent. By picking her, she could live more than one life.

The butterfly flew away, heading in the direction of the forest. Today, it looked welcoming, like Merlin had given all of his magic to enchant it. Through the immensity of the trees, I heard the engine of a car passing by. The ravens flew into the sky, not used to the sight of visitors, and the foliage stirred.

From a distance, I squinted at the red sports car stopping a few meters away from the gothic gate. A door slammed, and a man dressed in all white cut through the forest, not walking on the main path.

As he inched closer, fighting his way over with the wildness, I recognized his glowing blond hair and wide smirk. *Adonis.* He waved his hand at me, probably a sign to join him in the forest.

Without hesitation, I held my bouquet and ran in his direction with a smile. I opened the gate, which creaked with a shrill cry under the watching stare of the gargoyles guarding the property. I met Adonis half-hidden in the woods like he was a teenager going out after his curfew.

"What are you doing here?" I exclaimed.

"I came to see you, princess. We're friends, after all." His lips curved into a flirty grin, and he opened his arms.

He drew me into a caring hug, taking me fully under his embrace as if he had missed me for too long. I encircled one arm around him, the other protecting my bouquet from getting smashed against his torso. My head rested on his chest, and I smelled his purple scent, fading out with the overpowering scent of the flowers.

"It's good to see you." I pulled away.

The ocean blue of his eyes sparkled before he caught sight of my bouquet. "He's offered you flowers. He sure knows you well."

"It's actually for him. I picked them." I slammed my mouth shut, knowing how stupid that could sound.

"It's beautiful." Adonis swallowed harshly. "Even though I doubt he's refined enough to appreciate the view of beauty. Women should be the ones getting flowers."

The memory of the bouquet Adonis bought me last Christmas slipped through my mind, and an awkward silence washed over us. He took a deep breath, looking heavenward, his lips pressing together with a hesitation to tell me something.

"We didn't end our last phone call very well, and the last time we met at the opera, it was too brief. I wanted to see you in person. Things aren't going well for me," Adonis confided, his eyes glistening with phantoms that haunted him.

I took his hand, and I bored my eyes into his. "What's happening?"

"For starters, my father came back a couple of nights ago with a huge bruise on his face. Some dudes had beaten him up. Pricks. Those rats all want our money," he cursed. "And then, we had problems at the board. We're late on deliveries, and some of our investors troubled us." He passed his hand over his forehead, exhaling sharply. "Anyway, I'm sorry, I don't want to worry you with business."

My eyebrows lowered. "You know I'm here for you. I'm sorry about all that."

"I wish you could be here, Lily. . ." He leaned closer, his thumb stroking on my palm.

I smiled. "You're the heir of the biggest luxury goods company. Surely you can manage without me."

"Your uncle is worried too. He came to our place—he said you should be back home very soon. Is it true?"

The pounding of my heart echoed in my ears, and I instinctively took a step back. I didn't want to go back home. My uncle never mentioned his worries to me the day I messaged him to tell him I was close to making the aphrodisiac and have the perfume I for so long dreamed of achieving.

"He's missing you. He doesn't feel well." Adonis crossed his arms on his chest, his jaw clenching.

"Really?" Remorse burned the back of my throat, and panic surged through my veins. "Did something happen? Is it bad?"

"Yes." His stare hardened. My heart sank, imagining the worst of the scenarios until he added, "Yes, he misses you. He's lonely and depressed, but I've been there for him."

I nodded. "Thank you. I'll probably ask him if he wants to come to the manor."

A squawk of laughter jerked his head back. "You're joking, right?"

"Well, no," I bit out. "Radcliff may not be the most welcoming person…" *And he doesn't hold my uncle deep in his heart, but then again, he dislikes mostly everyone.* "But I don't see why not."

"For starters, he's not the type you introduce for a nice meal with your family." He raised a brow. "Second, he won't let you, Lily. Don't you see that you're like a prisoner here?"

"Adonis, please… Can't you see Radcliff has been good to me? Do I look different and unhappy to you?"

His eyes roamed my face, wandering across each of my features with a perplexed expression on his face. His stare latched onto my hair, and his nostrils flared.

"Cute brooch. Looks expensive," he quipped before heading back to his expensive car.

"Adonis—"

He interrupted me, his elbow leaning on the roof of his car with its door opened. "At Carmin, there will always be a place for you, princess. Good always wins against evil, right? You'll see."

He turned on the engine and gave me a last grin. But this one felt unnatural. It stretched out on his lips too deep to be true, and his eyes remained empty. I waved goodbye nonetheless, and he left the manor at blistering speed, pulling out the dust on the soil in a rising fog.

I coughed, the earthy smell prickling my nose and burning my throat as if I was being buried underground.

Fortunately, the smell of the bouquet brought me back to a colorful life, and I wondered if it would have the same effect on Radcliff.

"Radcliff?" I knocked at his office door for the third time.

Nothing.

I knocked again.

Still nothing.

Facing the silence, I turned away, surrendering to the evidence of his absence until a commanding voice penetrated my insides and froze me in place. "You can enter, Lily."

I lowered the handle and slid the door open. I hoisted myself into his office fashioned from shadows and the chill of wintry wind, a lullaby of moonlight that held the tale of lost souls.

Radcliff's shadow blanketed the cracking floor, the rays of the brindled light of dusk bypassing him. He was enthroned behind his wood desk, his spine straight and his palms further apart on each side of it. His face was closed off with merciless edges and his eyes impenetrable.

He rose from his regal silver-and-black leather chair, keeping his fists locked on the desk. He smoothed his tie and readjusted his five-piece suit, his eyes firmly set on my bouquet. He approached me with slow steps that echoed through the room to the point that the walls could shake with misery and misfortune.

"Flowers," he stated bitterly as if I was holding the most repellent of things.

A shiver scoured through my back like a heavy draft, telling me to escape. His hard stare fired at mine, and cold crept underneath my skin.

"Yes, it's a beautiful bouquet, right?" *Please, say yes.* I handed him the bouquet with moist, trembling hands, my heart slamming with apprehension. "What do you think?"

He seized the bouquet and observed it on each side with disdain. His lips twitched in an expression of disgust, and now I could only hear my heartbeats pounding in my ears. He clutched the fragile bouquet in a fist with all his strength and crushed the stems in his palm.

"What are you doing? You're gonna kill them!" I shrieked. "Stop!"

Pitiless, he ditched the bouquet on the ground like it was nothing, and a silent scream tore my insides. I dug my nails inside my palms, feeling as if there was a rift breaking my heart into small pieces.

Radcliff crushed the flowers under his foot, bleeding and killing them without an ounce of humanity.

"Noooo!" I fell to my knees, my strength vanishing under this massacre.

My chin shook, all my hopes vaporizing into the decaying air. The walls seemed to shrink away, and the coldness of the office stole my warmth, my heart decaying. With a trembling hand, I reached for the petals, but I retracted it, feeling my eyes glistening.

"Why did you do that?" I screamed, madness tinting my heart with its bitter colors. "Are you crazy?"

He didn't reply verbally, but a muscle in his jaw ticked. He was made of ruthless stone, shielding his heart from light and making sure nothing and no one would penetrate it.

I got up with a growing rage and spit the words with fury. "Why, Radcliff? Why would you—"

"*He* offered you those flowers." The harshness of his words was cruel.

The entire mansion reflected Radcliff. The frost on the window widened, as if it was imprisoning the manor, condemning it to coldness. Spirits huffed through the halls, a dark sigh of despair. The high-pitched cries of the taps, as if the water had been tainted with acid.

"What are you talking—" *Adonis.* My lips parted, mist escaping my mouth. "You saw Adonis and me today."

"I did," he ground out between clenched teeth, towering over me with all his terror. "I should make you pay for this."

"I think you already did." My temper sparked, glancing at the crushed flowers. The fresh swell of revenge rose in me like a tide and festered in me. "Plus, I can see whoever I want. You don't own me."

"Oh, but I do, little witch."

Before I could open my mouth to retort, he had pinned me against the wall, brimming with hostility. My stomach coiled. His hand gripped my throat, and the darkness in his raven eyes defied mine as the purple shades of chaos inside his gaze confronted the golden magic inside mine. His muscles tensed, and flames of anger licked through him like the most hellish fire.

"You're. Fucking. Mine," he articulated so close to my neck in a dangerous whisper, his fingers clasping on my waist. I was at his mercy. "You let him offer you those ridiculous flowers as if you were his, and on top of that, you made him come to my property. Don't fucking betray me like that ever again, or I'll kill him, and I'll deliver the picturesque scent of his corpse to you as a gift."

"What? I didn't even know he'd be here!" I locked my eyes firmly with his. "You have to believe me. He was worried—you misunderstood. I was just being a good friend, nothing more."

"And now, thanks to you, your little Junior will taste how it feels to defy me," he snarled with malicious glee, his lips sketching into a dark sneer.

His gaze dropped to the hold he had on me, then to my eyes. With gritted teeth, he released me from his grip and turned around, pacing back to his window. I released the breath I didn't know I was holding, shivers of bitterness running through my body.

"Leave," he ordered, his back facing me and the mist of his breath stretching against the glass.

I stayed in place, my nostrils flaring. At this moment, I hated him so much that I didn't know if he deserved the truth.

"Leave." His fist slammed on the glass, which cracked like scaly thorns and made me jump in fear. His profile with the scar faced me, revealing the monster in him. "For your own sake, listen to me."

My heart slowed, leaving me empty. My mouth went slack,

and my eyes glistened, witnessing the worst of his humanity burning him.

"He didn't even offer me those flowers," my voice slurred in a weary monotone. "I picked them for you, Radcliff..."

He turned around brutally with wide eyes. "What?"

"I picked each flower," I raged with venom, my chin and mouth trembling. "I wanted to offer you a gift just like you did for me. I selected each of them to show you how I see you. I thought you'd appreciate it. Clearly, I was wrong."

I thundered away from his office, my feet striking the ground, the lost souls of ghosts inside the manor for company.

Chapter 7

Radcliff

I threw away all the papers in my office and brought my fist to my chin, wanting to bite away the swell of rage tiring my guts. I cracked my head to the side and exhaled all the chaos I wanted—no, needed—to inflict. I contemplated the irony of the situation. The shattered window had taken the form of a sanguinary stained glass. Another sign of the monster in me.

A bitter aftertaste hung in my throat, the need to make Junior pay stronger than anything. He had already gotten on my nerves before, but the step he took today was a challenge. I imagined the sweet noise of his scream as I slaughtered his throat with the key to his pitiful car. I could do that. But I wouldn't. I had something tremendously bigger planned: humiliation.

Amusement flickered in the ghost of a smile. I needed to find the perfect punishment.

One thing was sure: he would pay for it.

One way or another.

See, Junior was the Moon. Anyone with common sense could have predicted it. It was the card of illusion and deception, and that prick was filled with disillusions—about his sinful father and mostly about craving what was mine. He simply couldn't admit the truth to himself.

My mind erased the thoughts about that worthless human at the sight of Lily running through the garden in the direction of the greenhouse. I pushed aside the curtains so I could see her better, my black heart tightening into a knot. I was responsible for her pain.

But that wasn't the worst part. With her, I was capable of the worst of humanity. There was no doubt I'd kill anyone for her. I'd have fucked her right away in my office, brutal and hard, like a beast in my quest to make her forget every other bastard. I'd have used her orgasms against her, making her forget every other man's name.

If one man dared to touch her or lay their perverted eyes upon her, I'd tear out either his eyes or his hands and send them to her as a reminder that she belonged to me. I'd ink my name on her, like a brand she would never get rid of.

I was thirsty to possess and own her, no matter which destruction I'd inflict. *She should have never been mine.*

I didn't like feeling jealous and *powerless.*

Those emotions were new to me, and—

"What the fuck is she doing?"

Lily was now inside the greenhouse, going back and forth with heavy steps. My eyes followed her movements; she seemed to ramble. Out of nowhere, she stopped and screamed at the Devil's Corpse by spewing a flow of words—probably cursed ones—I wished I could hear.

My lips curled into a thin line as I watched the spectacle that she was.

She moved her hands frantically and hysterically, talking to that flower as if she was complaining to her best friend. *Complaining about you, asshole.* She ran a hand through her hair and then listed something on her fingers. And hell, that list was long. It had five… six… seven points.

The last one was definitely the worst, judging by the way she tightened her fingers into a fist, like she wanted to squeeze something—probably my throat.

That witch was crazy.

I liked that.

To be honest, it even turned me on.

Lily finished her performance, craning her neck backward and shutting her eyes as if she was drained out of all her energy. She sat down at the roots of the flowers, continuing her confession, but this time, sadness clouded her features.

A muscle in my jaw tensed, and I jerked away from the window, pulling the curtain to keep the light out. The room faded in black velvet and emerald green, the peaceful silence of darkness cloaking the whispering stories of ashes and bones of the manor.

Truth was, I was an idiot.

I turned at the small portion of the destruction I had inflicted. The crushed flowers on my floor glared at me in their misery. I leaned over their drooping petals and bleeding stems.

Nobody's ever given me a gift.

People came to me for favors like I was fucking Santa, but no one had ever given me anything without expecting something in return. She had. And I tore that apart knowing far too well what flowers represented to her. She expressed herself through them and their scents.

I picked up the dying bouquet in my palm, the flowers' heads leaning in the direction of their graves. Out of something beautiful, I'd created something ugly. Out of a living thing, I'd created death. Everything I touched withered away.

I stepped out of my office, finding Cerba behind the doorstep. Our gazes locked, and she had the decency to bark at me.

"Move." I snapped my fingers, gesturing for her to descend down the stairs.

She barked again, wagging her tail. I creased my forehead, but her smile widened. She was the only living thing that stuck with me, and I had not the slightest idea why.

I stepped ahead of her. "I wonder sometimes if you're not a fucking ghost too."

Being haunted by the ghost of a dog with a tragic fate would make more sense. It was at this moment, Cerba decided to sprint down the stairs with all her living self, passing in front of me. I followed after her, on my way to the living room to search for Mrs. Walton.

Delight wasn't the expression on my face when I found her. Spasms of irritation crossed my features as I studied with a critical squint Mrs. Walton sewing some sort of old sock on *my* leather couch. It was ugly. Not useful. And I was paying her for doing that useless shit.

That old shrew turned gray and immediately rose up at the sound of my thundering footsteps on the ground. She hid her tools on the sofa as if I hadn't witnessed the horrible piece of wool or whatever she was sewing.

"I'll have dinner with Lily tonight," I stated. "Eight sharp."

She nodded, her gaze bulging from her sockets with too many questions at the bouquet I was holding. I dropped it onto the sofa instinctively, clearing my throat.

"I'm not paying you to stand here. Go." I sharpened my eyes murderously, and hers stared at me in a catatonic stupor.

She picked up her sock—unless it was a faceless creepy doll—in a hurry and then went to pick up the dead flowers.

"Don't."

She jolted, her gaze shifting between me and the flowers.

I turned my back to her. "Leave them."

LILY

"I'm not sure I should go." I twirled the dinner invitation between my fingers. "Men are so stupid sometimes. Am I right?"

I lifted my head, my gaze searching through the Devil's Corpse crimson petals for an answer. She had bloomed, to the point that she masked several panes of the roof, soaring toward the sky. Her thorns, like sharp teeth, bristled on her flytraps. Her stems, like tentacles, seemed to have a heartbeat, keeping her alert to everything that was happening around her.

"Radcliff and I, it's…" I drew a shaky breath, thinking of the right words. "Uncanny."

My eyebrow raised. "Twisted."

My gaze dropped to Cerba, crouching at my feet. Her eyes glistened at me, her tail jumping from one side to another. "Magical."

I snorted, shaking my head. "Unlikely."

I rose up, removing dirt from my dress. I passed my fingers through the dry tears inked on my cheek and inhaled the powerful scent of folklore tales and dark velvet dreams.

"Wish me luck," I said with determination.

I felt the vines of the Devil's Corpse brushing on my arm, their caress encouraging me to face Radcliff.

"Thank you." I shot a last glance at my flower with the deepest smile and ambled toward the exit of the greenhouse. "Let's go, Cerba."

She ran wildly in the direction of the manor, and I followed after her in the midst of the night. Shivers spread on my skin hearing the howling cries of the owls and the haunting shrieks of the ravens. My heart galloped in my chest, my footsteps hastening on the grass, for fear a midnight monster would catch up to me.

Behind the gothic stained glass windows, a golden light shimmered into the dining room area, contrasting with the surrounding darkness. I passed through the entrance door and arrived face-to-face with Mrs. Walton, her hands crossed in front of her belly. She tapped her watch twice on her wrist with her finger, letting me know I was late, if her severe and hostile stare wasn't warning enough.

"Well, he'll just have to wait for me." I arched an eyebrow, keeping my composure. I was probably just five minutes late; it wouldn't be the end of him.

She hesitated, observing me as if I was a specimen straight out of a mental asylum. She then readjusted some strands of my hair, making it fall over my breasts. She tried to smooth my dress by hiding the folds of it. She probably feared my lack of "style" would displease Radcliff. A smile lightened my face at the thought.

Mrs. Walton finally let me go, and I crossed the empty, cold hallway to step toward the light with my chin lifting proudly. But my heart and pride sank to my feet at the view of Radcliff.

He sat in his usual regality at the end of the grand oval table, the flames of the fireplace rising behind him like the hellfire in him. His jaw was tight, his eyes burning mine. He tapped his card on the wood table.

We couldn't be more opposite. He smelled of elegance and of all the richness in the universe while I smelled of spring blossom and potting soil. He was proper in a pitch-black suit that left no place for imperfections while I was a mess.

I shot a glance at the watch around Radcliff's wrist. *Fuck.* I was late. Half an hour late. I swallowed the bad feeling creeping up my spine.

"Take a seat, Lily." He spoke calmly, probably to keep the torrent of anger lashing through him in check.

The gastronomic dishes were untouched.

The gothic chandeliers were lit up on the table, their wax already dripping down.

Radcliff had waited for me.

"I shouldn't have been late." I took place in my seat, my heart blooming at the intention.

"You've made your point." His eyes closed on mine, dark with chaos and haunted with starved demons, before his lips pressed into a thin line.

"No, I didn't do it on purpose. I was—"

The words from my mouth escaped into a soundless gasp. A vase, or more likely a very expensive and historical antique, was placed at the center of the table.

It carried inside of it my bouquet.

Or rather an assembly of crushed flowers.

My nostrils flared, my eyes widening and my mouth slamming shut. I shifted my gaze to Radcliff, a horde of chills scouring my skin. He held mine, hiding his discomfort as much as he could by maintaining an impenetrable expression, confronting the shock in mine.

Our eyes locking into something that intense and intimate could only mean *that* was his doing. He had put water inside the vase that was meant to never be touched, trying to repair the damage he had caused. Our souls spoke the words we were too proud to admit.

Most flowers looked down, halfway caught between life and death. A wooden stick was in the center, trying to hold them together.

It was awkward.

A light smile curved my lips. I could tell he had no idea what he was doing, but this showed the Devil I knew cared.

"Why did you fix them?" I whispered, my emotions lowering the timbre of my voice.

"Because they make me think of you."

That was it. Just a statement that sent my cells dancing, and the butterflies in my belly flew widely. Just a statement that resurrected my core and made my heart pump all the blood it could. Just a statement that set me aflame, heat coursing down my center. He had said the words I wanted to hear, giving me the reassurance I needed.

I displayed a smile and put my napkin on my lap as we were about to start our dinner. My gaze fell on the food served—in particular, the desserts—placed on a silver tray to my left.

Macarons of all colors. There was the champagne-flavored one, which was my uncle's favorite. I used to get a box of them every year for his birthday. A cloud of sadness washed over my face at the memory, the words of Adonis haunting me with regret.

"Something is on your mind." Radcliff's voice made me snap back to reality.

"It's nothing. Just the macarons. I—" I sunk my eyes inside his obsidian ones. I couldn't hide anything from him, even if the moment was misplaced. "Can I ask you something?"

He roamed my face, probably trying to read my mind. "Of course."

"Can I…" I played with my fork, a feeling of unease traveling through my veins. "Can I invite my uncle to the manor?"

A frown drew his eyebrows together. "Why would you want that?"

"Because he's my uncle," I quipped back. "He's my only family."

"The one that abandoned you here. He didn't seem to care before." He dropped his napkin to his knees, his hand tensing into a fist as he hissed bitterly, "You don't need that kind of family."

My heart leaped to my throat. "You don't know him like I do. I miss him."

Plus, I hoped my uncle would see Radcliff like I did. Eugene was the only one alive with whom I could confide my feelings about the perfume.

Mrs. Walton served the food, the silver cutlery hitting the porcelain plates the only noise to fill the void. She took her leave right after Radcliff's dismissive wave of his hand. He poured the wine inside our cups, and I brought the scallops infused with white wine and mushroom purée to my lips.

A muscle tightened in his jaw as he said, "Very well, then."

"Really?" My lips parted, and I dropped the fork and the scallop on my plate.

"It's important to you." He gripped his wineglass, spinning the bloodred liquid. "But your uncle doesn't deserve this."

"Thank you. I know you're not really fond of him." *But perhaps you could change your mind about him.*

A cruel and sinister snarl tilted his lips. "I know the darkness in every human, Lily. Their vices, fears, cravings, and sins. My judgment is always right."

"How?" *How did you become the Devil?*

"How do you have the gift of smell?" He emptied his glass, and for a moment, I wanted to be this red liquid settling on his lips. "For the simple reason that I'm born this way just as you're born that way."

We'd been cursed with a blessing in disguise.

Our pasts had been dark, and I wondered if Radcliff had been an outsider just like me. If we had shared the same pain and loneliness, being stuck in the shadows at the mercy of demons.

"How was it?" I was eager to ask. "Growing up. How did you know?"

"Darkness has been my… friend. It called out to me. Do you

hear it sometimes?" His eyes blazed at mine, reflecting the hungry flames rising inside them.

"No…" I took my first bite, knowing I needed to get closer to the point where he had lost his humanity. "But I speak to flowers." *Or perhaps we're both mentally insane.* "How were you as a child?"

"Short story, I brought chaos and destruction to everyone that dared to approach me," he deadpanned. "I read the darkest part of them."

My heartbeats slowed. "And the long story?"

A sly grin curved his lips into obscure features. "You'll not want to eat after that tale."

"I don't care." I let go of the fork that hit my plate and intertwined my clammy hands together, playing with my thumbs. "I want to hear it."

"My father used to host Bible studies in the exact same room we're in," he stated, his eyes creeping through the room as if the memory was engraved in the air. "He invited to his table the most important and powerful men. All good churchmen, of course. I must have been no more than ten when I had to attend those boring meetings. My mother, well, she was playing hostess. A hostess who wore only long sleeves to hide her bruises."

The flames of the chandeliers crackled, and a frozen chill caressed my back. Radcliff's eyes twisted with malice, and his finger traced the curve of his glass, making it sing like a ghost fiddle.

"My father said she was… clumsy. He also made sure I wouldn't cause a scene. I was ordered to sit straight on my chair, not move an eyebrow, and speak only when I was asked to. I was a ghost child, my father making sure to refute rumors that I was cursed by feeding them lies. But you see, all of his guests, portraying the righteousness, the spokespersons of goodness, had black souls. The man to his right was cheating on his wife with prostitutes, defrauding his employees, and the man to his left was a porn addict who beat his wife. How did I know that? At first, it was just an instinct. I could perceive the color of their souls and the evilness around them. Their cravings. I could confuse them and get them to reveal their true colors to me."

I imagined young Radcliff, with his solemn, cold air, staying mute and already giving the creeps to the sinners. Perhaps this was what the aphrodisiac was about? Peeling the mask off those who had wronged him.

"My father was reading the verse 1 Peter 4:8 to my mother in front of his guests. *Most important of all, continue to show deep love for each other, for love covers—*"

"A multitude of sins," I finished.

Our eyes locked. He had probably been assigned to learn the verses of the Bible as I had to at the institute of the young ladies. *His mother's bruises.* This verse wasn't a declaration of love; it was either a demand for forgiveness or a promise it'd continue like that.

"He kept on reciting verses of love, all as false as each other, so I said in the middle of this assembly of deceitful humans: 'you're all liars.' They all fell silent after that, staring at the monster that I was. The dead ruling over this wicked atmosphere." Radcliff's grin became cunning. "He didn't take it well, but he'd never punish me in front of them. No, he'd wait, as twisted as he was. His friends began to advise him on the subject of me. The homeschooled child who scared away each teacher he had. The one without a soul. That's when the biggest sinner of them all spoke, suggesting a psychiatric asylum or deep cleansing."

Unable to drag my eyes away from Radcliff and being swallowed by his gloomy story, I asked, "What did you say? What did—"

"You. Tried. To. Molest. Me."

Radcliff pronounced this sentence without an ounce of emotion, his harsh words making the flames flicker. My heart sank, and I remained like marble. He had taken my voice with him.

"That noble churchman had pictures of children and was an

abuser. Obviously, no one believed the weak, scared child that I was. Well…" His lips pressed into a thin line, his eyes gleaming with chaos. "Not until I made the hierophant pay by showing his true face to the light, but that's another story."

"Radcliff, it's terrible… I had no idea, I—" My forehead creased, the words getting stuck in my throat. "You didn't deserve this. No one deserves to live this. What did your parents do?"

"My father killed the 'crows of misfortunes,' as he called them, that I had adopted. He poisoned them. Made me watch. Then, he continued his experiments on me to erase that darkness inside me. My mother usually stepped aside. She had her own misery to take care of."

"It's not a curse," I hedged, my eyebrow slanting inward, facing that ugliness. My hand curved into a fist, my nails digging down my palms. "Some flowers bloom in the dark under the moon. You were made a monster, but you're so much more. You have a gift."

"She said the same thing." Radcliff cleared his throat.

"I hate your father. I wish for him to burn in hell." I spat the words with hatred, closing my eyes firmly. "He's horrible."

"Oh, he got what he deserved, be assured." A ghost of a smile spread on his lips.

"What do you mean?"

"He died." His smile grew even more terrible and wicked. "And I can assure you, it was anything but pleasurable."

I released the air I was holding, and the candles blew up into smoke. A fire burnt my stomach under the realization. I was on Radcliff's side, accepting that villainous act he did. It wasn't only a confession; it was a test of what rules he was ready to bow and which torture he could inflict.

And that didn't bother me.

On the contrary, I understood him.

"Good," I said, my eyes celebrating with the darkness in his own.

He raised his glass of wine in another toast.

"But why are you like that with me, then?" I gulped, wondering why he was accepting me, showing me a kindness he never did to anyone else. Couldn't he read my darkness?

"You already know the answer deep inside of you, flower goddess." He rose from his seat, looming toward me with all his dark aura. "I know you better than you know yourself."

The fire inside of me built up, consuming me whole, stinging my body. "What does that mean?"

He leaned on the table a few inches from me, his whisper so close to my neck. "We were fated."

He seized my hand, directing me to stand up. And with a caress on my cheek, he promised:

"I'll be a monster to everyone else but never to you, Lily."

Chapter 8

Radcliff

Having an imposter at my manor wasn't on my program. The desire to kill him on the spot had crossed my mind. The idea of it grew more and more appealing as the minutes passed by. Consideration flickered in my eyes and disappeared at the view of Lily already in front of the gate. She was too impatient; it'd only cause her disillusion. Cerba remained at my side by the entrance, sitting like the guard dog that she was.

"And here we go." I exhaled, stubbing my cigar out on the floor.

Cerba jerked her ears back, hearing the sound of the impostor's car passing through the forest. Even she was confused. I took heavy steps on the grass. Cracked my knuckles. Readjusted my diamond cuffs. Snapped my gaze at the squawking ravens on the gargoyles.

My mind played tricks on me, manifesting the torture sound of a church hymn carrying on the air, contrasting with Lily's bright smile. I inhaled the melody, my expression turning brisk and businesslike despite the fact that inside I was bitterly regretting my choice.

"Wait inside, Lily. I need to speak with your uncle first." I couldn't help the spasms of irritation crossing my face.

She frowned as if she had a choice. I thought she'd complain, but that little witch's hair swayed with the wind, infusing her floral scents into the air.

She spellbound me, drawing a playful smile with malicious eyes. "Don't frighten him too much, please."

Has she seen her coward of an uncle? That fool was afraid of everything—he didn't have an ounce of bravery.

She arched an eyebrow. My thoughts were too loud. A thin line drew on my lips. Looked like the little witch was getting to know me. Lily then walked away in the direction of the manor, jumping from one foot to the other, Cerba joining her. *So much for a guard dog.*

The fool's car parked in front of the opened gate, and I repressed the urge to torture him. The view of the impostor getting out of his piece of crap didn't help my urges. That foolish smile with trembling lips. His shoulders curving inward like he was the Hunchback of Notre Dame. His grayish hair and the food crumbs on his vest. How did Lily have patience with such a pitiful human? She was a saint.

He searched for his niece—if he thought I'd let Lily welcome him, he was insane. I was the owner of the manor, and his invitation didn't guarantee he'd pass my gates.

I had rules he'd need to bow to if he wished to see his niece.

"Radcliff… Thank you for welcoming me here. You're very clement."

Don't kill him.

Don't kill him.

I repeated it like a mantra.

"I brought something…" He handed me a bottle of wine. Cheap wine.

A nerve in my jaw twitched as I lost my patience.

When I didn't budge, he put the bottle on his car's seat and cleared his throat. With a trembling voice, he dared to speak again. "Can I see my niece?"

He made the wrong move of stepping forward, and I grabbed his neck, sending his body banging against the gate. The heavy noise echoed, the crows and their shrill cries soaring in the sky.

Eugene's eyes widened, his face ghostly white. The helpless bug was trapped by the monstrous spider.

"Let me make something clear, Eugene." I clamped down on his neck, enough for him to struggle for his breath, not hard enough *yet* so he'd choke his blood. "If you upset me or Lily, I'll end your miserable life without thinking twice. I'll cut the blood vessels in your nostrils with a sharp knife until you bleed to death."

My lips curled into a snarl, terrifying enough for his chin to tremble. I released my grip, and he dropped down onto the ground. He coughed, stroking his neck. I readjusted my suit, and he took his sweet time to lift himself up.

"Lily," he stammered in a suffocated whisper. "Who is she to you?"

"She's mine." When repulsion twitched on his face, I had to add, "Everything about her is."

That's right, old man. I took her virginity and soul.

"Promise me you won't hurt her…"

Look who pretends to care.

"You lost the right to care for her after what you did." That secret he willingly exchanged for saving his meaningless life.

"I didn't mean to do that… I didn't have a choice back then and—"

"You always have a choice, and now it's a secret you'll bury in your grave. You won't be able to repent from your sins, and you can be damn sure I'll be in hell to torment you." The truth was too painful for Lily to hear. Plus, I was taking care of it—my role was to shield her from the outside world.

"I'll never tell her." Eugene shook his head. "I'll never hurt my Lily."

"You better not, or I'll do worse than kill you."

LILY

"Mrs. Walton is such a good cook! Everything looked so luxurious. I—" My uncle exhaled with a smile. "I can understand why you're not eager to go back home."

"It's not for the food." I chuckled, and we continued our way across the garden.

My uncle's scent of newspaper and amber filled my nostrils. Cerba kept her distance, following behind us by a few steps. Since the day he left me at Ravencliff Manor, this was the first moment we'd been alone, and yet, we'd barely talked since he arrived.

He had devoured the food, as if he hadn't eaten a real meal for weeks, and spent his focus mostly on trying to guess Mrs. Walton's recipe for filet mignon. Radcliff didn't join us; I hadn't seen him since he went to greet my uncle. I wasn't surprised, though. He valued each second of his time, and he didn't hold my uncle close in his heart.

"You look beautiful." Uncle truly set his eyes upon me, caressing a strand of my hair. "Your hair looks darker."

"Thank you. I'm so happy that you're here." I hooked an arm

around his, leading him to the bench facing the greenhouse. I could finally share my excitement about my special place with someone.

"I've missed you." Uncle narrowed his eyes in defiance at the manor. "How's everything going with him and that… thing?"

"It's a flower, Uncle, not a thing." Thinking about Radcliff, a crimson blush tinted my cheeks, and a beam lit up my features. "Radcliff and I, we have gotten closer, and I—"

"You slept with him?" My uncle's jaw ticked in disapproval as he removed my arm wrapped around his to take a seat on the bench. His gaze closed on the greenhouse, like a child sulking on my decision.

I ignored my thumping heart and switched the subject. He probably knew the answer anyway.

"I can't believe you'd never told me about this greenhouse." I sat next to him, searching for a flicker of happiness in his eyes. "It's pure heaven. And the Devil's Corpse? It's something else entirely."

"You definitely brightened the place from the last time I came here."

Cerba sat at my feet and growled at Eugene. She showed her canines, her nose wrinkling. Her eyes darkened with defiance. She didn't trust my uncle yet.

"Cerba doesn't like strangers, I'm sorry." I petted her, trying to reassure her, talking to her in a small voice. "He won't hurt you, cutie, okay?"

"She has three legs." Uncle frowned. "I've never seen that dog before."

It seemed like the manor held many mysteries, as if a cloud of black smoke was hiding the truth. A cloud that could be crossed by only a selection of individuals that could seek its most hidden secrets.

Uncle took my hand, leaning forward. "Did you make his… demand?"

"Yes." I nodded proudly with a thin smile. "I did it, Uncle. At least, I think I did. And the perfume I made, it's like nothing else I've ever scented. It's a masterpiece."

"Congratulations, my Lily." He hugged me tight before stroking my cheek with the kind of love a father has for his child. "Your mother would be so proud. You can come back home now."

Sadness washed away my smile, a bad feeling twitching my stomach. "I don't know, Uncle… I mean, yes, someday, but I—"

"You can have your dream." His eyes sparkled, and he lowered his voice to a whisper, his stare shifting on every corner like someone about to tell a forbidden gossip. "I spoke to Christian Carmin. I'm trying to have him on our side."

"What do you mean?" The hair on my skin raised in alert— that would explain why Adonis and my uncle had been close lately.

"Your perfume," he continued eagerly. "We could sell it to him! He'll be interested to meet with you about it. And in exchange, you could be a nose for Carmin. Think of all the gains we could make!"

There wasn't a we.

There was only an I.

I made all of this happen. It was thanks to me. Not him. Not Christian. Not anyone.

My nostrils flared. I'd never dreamed of working for someone. I wanted to build my own kingdom, not live in someone else's.

"That's why you're here?" I questioned, a feeling of bitterness like a corrosive liquid making my throat ache. I was hurt he would choose business and his personal gains over me. *Again.*

"Of course not. I'm trying to think about what's good for you. For example, you should reconnect with Adonis. He's been good to you. The poor kid misses you."

"Because he's a Carmin?" I raised an eyebrow and snorted, shaking my head in disbelief.

"No, Lily—"

Eugene tried to get closer, but Cerba stood up and barked at him angrily. She wanted to protect me as if she could feel the dark emotions building up inside of me.

"What is she doing?" Eugene slid back from the bench.

"Cerba, I'm fine. Stop this." But she didn't stop.

She took another step forward, barking with hostility at my uncle. She wanted him out. To scare him. She'd never hurt—

"Be quiet!" Eugene kicked her out, throwing her away from him.

"Cerba!" I screamed, rushing to her side.

Her tail was between her legs, her ears tilted back. I dropped on the grass and scooped her between my arms, searching to see if she was hurt. She gave me a sweet look and licked my arm to reassure me.

"I'm sorry, Lily. I didn't mean to do that to her. I got scared," Eugene excused himself, his hands pleading and his eyes opening wide in shock. The smell of sweat and weakness raked all over him.

"You should go, Uncle." My stare sent venom at him.

"Lily, please," he excused again with that shaking voice of his.

"She's Radcliff's dog. If he knew what you did to his dog, he wouldn't be pleased. If you leave now, I won't tell."

He nodded, fear eating him alive. "I'm sorry."

You're a coward, Uncle.

He left without another word, afraid of the consequences. He had always given up on me because he was possessed with fear. All of his life, he had made bad decisions because he couldn't take risks and didn't believe in himself—nor in me. He was weak, and that was the reason he couldn't love me like I wanted him to.

I simpered, dropping Cerba on the grass as she put her paw on my arm, boring her eyes into me. "Thank you for protecting me. But I don't want you to hurt yourself, okay?"

She rubbed her nose against my elbow and wailed.

"I'm fine," I promised as tears welled up the corners of my eyes. "I'll be fine."

I looked heavenward, hoping to hold my tears back, but I shut my eyes and let them drop like a hot torrent. I calmed down my breath, focusing on the odors of my surroundings. It smelled of the earthy green and blossoming pink spring, apart from… Sandalwood. Vanilla. Patchou—

Cerba ran away from me, and I whirled around. Radcliff was behind me, and when his gaze roamed my face, his brows slanted downward. His eyes glowed with savage fire. I tried to erase the tears, but it was too late—he had seen them. The veins in his neck stood out in livid ridges, and his mouth twitched inward.

We locked eyes.

Waited.

And then, he growled like a beast on the hunt, and he left.

"Radcliff, no!" I yelled after him.

I ran to catch him as fast as I could, knowing him well enough to know he was on his way to inflict chaos and devastation. I wrapped my arms around his back, catching myself on him without thinking to force him to stop. It worked nevertheless. I laid my head against his costume, feeling all of his muscles stiffening.

"Please. I don't want you to cause my uncle any problems. He didn't do anything to me. He's my family, and I could never live with myself if anything were to happen to him."

"Let me go, Lily," he hissed.

"Don't go after him, because I promise you, if you hurt him, I'll cry for the rest of my life, and that would be because of you." I swallowed, whispering the last words. "Don't break my heart."

He turned around, and I saw the conflict rising inside his purple calla lily eyes. I begged him with my soul, hoping this time someone would choose me and my needs over hurting me with their own emotions.

Muscles flicked angrily in his jaw. "And I'll make you another promise, Lily."

I waited in a daze, a shiver coursing down my spine.

He loomed closer, his shadow swallowing me whole in his darkness. "I'll make every person who makes you cry pay. Even kill if I have to."

I know. "I'd never want that."

"Now, tell me what happened," he demanded.

"Promise me you won't do anything if I tell you?"

"That depends."

I shot him a frozen glare.

"Nothing drastic."

"You won't hurt my uncle?" I let myself be carried away by the wind toward the cliff, passing in front of the greenhouse. "And you have to promise."

"I said," he gritted his teeth, following me, "nothing drastic."

Well, it's better than expected.

I sat on the grass, keeping a safe distance from the edge of the cliff, the salty air filling my nostrils as the waves crashed on the hard rocks.

"My uncle, he has this kind of obsession with the Carmins. He admires them so much. I feel that he wishes to be them, you know?" I intertwined my fingers together, playing with them. "He thinks he knows what's best for me. He put them on a pedestal, but if only he knew the truth."

I craned my neck at Radcliff, not believing I was choosing him to confide in. His Adam's apple bobbed, betraying the fact he was trying to maintain his self-control for me. His expression was severe and screamed of everything but empathy. He, nonetheless, sat next to me on the grass, adjusting his suit.

"What truth." His voice itched with wrath, begging to be unleashed.

I exhaled shakily. "Once, I was at Adonis's place, and his dad… he was more than friendly with me. He tried to—" I rubbed my fingers together, my throat tightening. I had to get the words out now, or they would get stuck. "Touch me, but I pulled away. I thought I misinterpreted everything back then, but I always had a bad feeling about him, and now, seeing my uncle so close to him, well…"

My nose wrinkled at the spicy scent of this memory trying to haunt me again. I pushed it away, letting the woody scent of Radcliff be my safe haven.

Everything about him was calm and placid except for the vein popping out on his forehead and the vessels of his eyes reddening to the same color of his scar. He was boiling. Suddenly it was cold, as if every shadow in the world heard his silent call and snuggled against him, ready to terrorize the earth.

"Touch you where?" He was emotionless, his ruthless voice leaving no room to challenge his authority.

"Nothing happened. We just misunderstood each other, that's it."

My lips curved into a light smile, instantly dispelled by Radcliff's merciless gaze ordering me to continue the story.

"I was waiting for Adonis inside his living room when Christian entered wearing only a half-open bathrobe. White with his initials sewn on." My eyebrows knitted together, my stare falling upon my hands. "He was charming, complimenting me as he got closer to me. The next minute, his fingers skimmed over my arm, and I took a step back and was caged against the wall. But he wasn't rough or brutal, no… He was smiling, confident. It was easy for him, like all of this was normal. Perhaps I'd sent him signals he wrongly interpreted, I don't know."

I swallowed the new knot forming in my throat. "Of course, I was uneasy, but what could I have said? I wanted to be polite, and I hadn't encountered many men before. I didn't want to accuse him of something I misinterpreted." My lips pursed together. "He knew how to turn all of this, to get what he wanted. I felt his… thing pulsing against me. He offered to meet him later so we could talk about perfume. He said he could help me, and during this whole time, his hand had traveled to my butt. For a few seconds, I didn't understand nor move. I eventually pulled back and left their house."

"I own people like Carmin because of their weakness and their vices. Their mistakes always benefited me," Radcliff admitted, his gaze stuck on the horizon. "But not when it's about you. He won't touch you ever again." His eyes, surrounded by shadows, captured mine. "Which hand was it? Do you want me to deliver it to you?"

"What?" I shrieked. "Are you kidding?"

He wasn't.

His expression didn't move, and a deadly stillness took possession of him.

"No, of course, no. I don't want you to cut off his hand. It's…" A creepy shiver slithered through my veins. "Monstrous."

Chaos flickered in his eyes. "Just like him. It's a fair judgment."

"No, I—" I shook my head. "Let's change the subject, please." I brushed him off with a smile.

His silence haunted my thoughts. My heart tightened in my chest under his heavy stare. I was afraid of his next words.

"Whatever pleases you." He surprised me, my heart thanking him for eclipsing the subject. "If you had to choose a place to be right now, where would you be? Think of a happy memory."

"I'd be in Grasse in a flower field. The dreamland of perfumers." A smile grew on my face as I imagined myself dancing across the diverse blooms and scents on a scorching sun. "I never went there, but my mother and uncle grew up there. It was her dream to return back to Grasse with me one day. We said we would have our typical Mediterranean house and our little perfume shop. We even had a name for it. Well, I found the name." I laughed at the thought.

"I was so young, and I used to wear a crown of flowers on my head every day, so I named our future shop the Flower Queens."

"It's a regal name, and truly accurate." Radcliff analyzed each trait of my face as if he wanted to memorize every inch of it.

"Yeah, it was." I chuckled, my hands traveling over the grass. "What about you?"

"I don't have such stories to tell."

"Well, can you at least tell me a story?" My eyes begged him.

"I know about the three gates of hell."

Well, it wasn't what I was expecting, but that'll do.

"It's more of a legend," he added.

"I want to hear it. Can you tell me?" I posed my head on his lap and laid the rest of my body on the grass in the fetal position, watching the sun descend on the water.

His body tensed, probably not used to this display of affection. Nonetheless, he rested his hand on my arm in a protective touch, shielding me from the outside world and demons wanting to consume me. I bit my lower lip at the feel of his growing hardness inside his trousers.

"The first one," he started, "is the cliff of Ravencliff. The legend believed it'd be a direct gate to the Styx River. The second is an island named Erebus, whose tall walls surround the island and keep anyone from accessing it. The only way is through a cave engulfed underwater. The swamp does not descend until each full moon, leaving a passage for the most courageous. It houses the most sumptuous jewels. And the last one, undiscovered by anyone, is a garden hosting a pomegranate tree, where the fruit would deliver direct access to the elysian fields."

"Do you think they exist?" The rays tried to persist, the sun almost hidden by the ocean. "Are all those legends real?"

The darkness swallowed the rays, letting the twilight rise.

"Oh, they're very much real."

Chapter 9

Radcliff

"Have you heard?"

Hugo and I both knew I had. The news was all over France. I lit my cigar and inhaled its bitter, metallic taste of ashes. It was like inhaling the essence of death itself. It calmed down the fresh swell of anger, its grayish color warming my bowels. Carmin's enterprise would launch a new branch in their luxury pseudo-empire. *Jewels.* They'd collaborate with celebrities, using the most superficial of marketing strategies.

That was his way of responding to the way I'd bought out parts of his silent investors and made it my personal goal to make his enterprise crumble to dust. It was the first step of the bloody revenge

I had concocted for him. I'd take everything from him. Slowly. Painfully. Evilly.

We started a game of chess, but only one of us had the potential for a checkmate—with only a king and a queen, I could annihilate all of his pawns combined.

For the third time, he had hurt Lily, and for that—

"Radcliff," Hugo called again, calming the hot torrent of lava ravaging my cells.

The smoke twirled across my office, like shades whispering to me the steps to follow. The reflection of my sinister snarl on my club's window was just a glimpse at the onyx horror dripping down my blood.

I would destroy *The Emperor*.

He craved to take what was mine.

He was playing god in my element.

"Well." I stubbed the cigar out on the floor, crushing it under my shoe the way I'd crush him. It left a hole in my wooden parquet, but all I saw was his grave.

I cracked my knuckles and faced Hugo. Impatient as always, he tapped his foot nervously on the ground, his arms crossed in anticipation of action, his eyes ready to latch onto anyone sinful. Not that I'd complain—his beryl-red energy was useful to me.

"That would be a shame if he didn't have any supplier to deliver him either precious rocks or metals," I stated with calmness, knowing that the perfect revenge was demanding patience and a dark, twisted heart.

After all, Carmin was all about luxury—when it wasn't for sex affairs, child labor, and slavery. Point was, I owned most of the mines, from gold to diamond and minor qualities. This meant he'd have to find another supplier other than me, and hell help me, he wouldn't find any.

"What are you talking about?" Hugo leaned on his shoulder on the window with an angry wolf's smirk on his face.

"What if the rocks were to be missing, let's say at the port." My stare hardened at Hugo, all my demons ready to be freed, flying to Earth to inflict sweet chaos. "After all, piracy still does exist and is more present than we would think."

"Piracy?" Hugo raised an eyebrow.

"I have contacts everywhere, Hugo. Just make the calls." I turned around to end the topic, facing my guests. "How do you think I've become the Devil?"

That was the thing about favors. They could be collected at any moment.

"Anything else?"

I was glad he asked.

"Did you know Mrs. Walton had a newfound passion for sewing?"

He snorted. "The point?"

"I want her to make something for me." I tore up a piece of paper, writing down the instructions to follow. "Give her this."

He seized the paper and didn't bother to hide his shock reading it. With his eyebrows raised, he laughed sarcastically. "Shit, it's madness."

A vile, deadly smile inked on my lips. "And you haven't heard the best part of it."

The unpleasant noise of heels clapping on the floor interrupted us. That symphony made my ears whistle the divine judgment that needed to be done to her. I shut my eyes, breathing deep to prepare myself for the storm to come.

"Radcliff!" Melissa barged into my office, unannounced— which was bold and very regrettable on her part.

I wasn't surprised, though. But for once, her timing couldn't be more perfect. Too bad for her, she wouldn't be able to assume the consequences of her actions.

"Huh, Melissa, we're having a discussion here," Hugo spat. "Don't you have work to do other than dress up like a freak show?"

"Chill, Hugo. It's not my fault you didn't bang anyone today. I just need to talk to Radcliff," she quipped back.

"For fuck's sake, Melissa, you don't have any—"

My knuckles cracked, and impatience seared my veins like a corrosive liquid.

"Hugo, let us alone. We'll continue this discussion later." I brimmed with hostility, turning around, tired of their childish behavior.

Melissa was glaring with glory, both of her arms settling on her hips. Hugo swallowed and nodded in frustration. He then took his leave, stomping the ground in heavy clomps.

"Melissa, I'm pleased that you're here." On my "pleased," she furrowed her brows. No doubt, she wasn't that stupid—she knew something was off.

She folded her arms, her sudden confidence vanishing. "Where is Christian?"

"Gone." My lips curled in a thin line. "He won't step a foot in my club, ever."

"Why?" She raised her voice in a capricious shrill, with an overdramatic hand gesture. "Was it because I liked him? Are you jealous?"

"The world doesn't revolve around you, Melissa."

She threw herself on the sofa, her eyes studying me with a critical squint, attempting to read another meaning between my words. Then, they glimmered with twisted hope. "I don't understand you."

"Perhaps you'll understand this?" I went to my desk to pick up a contract and dropped it on the table facing her.

She seized it with her manicured fingers immediately. Her

venomous little eyes widened at first with excitement, but when she finally read what was written inside, her expression shifted to disgust with a grim and tight mouth, her stare blazing murderously at the piece of paper. It was priceless.

"What's all this?" she yelled, shaking the contract before jerking it on the ground, as if that would help her case.

A ghost of a smile teased the corners of my lips. "A reassignment."

She had spoken to Lily. She had given her access to that red room, knowing what would happen to her with those pricks. She had thrown her under the claws of sinners, hoping they'd break her with their vicious touch. I had warned her not to mess with her, and she went against my orders anyway. Her soul had always been twisted despite the fact that she was a lost one, and this time, she was beyond redemption.

"I already have a job here!" She rose up, hysterical. "I'm no bathroom cleaner, Radcliff! Can you see me doing that?"

No, that's why you'll be perfect.

She pointed a shaking finger in the direction of the ceiling, her tongue rolling inside her mouth.

"You need me here—you can't do this. You won't find anyone else who presents like me," she said, trying to convince herself before gesturing hysterically over her body. "This body doesn't scream toilet cleaner!"

I towered over her threateningly, already bored of this short amusement. "Either you take my offer to work as the cleaning lady of my club *forever*, or you leave. And let me tell you, no one will employ you. I'll make sure of that."

"Why are you doing this?" she whined.

She would cry if she wasn't so proud. If there was one thing Melissa hated the most in the universe, it was to be hidden from the spotlight. That was the most torturous price to pay for her. It was a public humiliation. That was the best punishment. Contrary to what people thought, death wasn't the ultimate price to pay; it was too easy.

"I warned you that if you ever talked to Lily or hurt her ever again that you'd pay the price."

"But I—"

"You'll like the uniforms." I pulled away from her. "They're orange, exactly like the ones in prison."

⚜

The middle of the night was an exquisite symphony.

For some people, it was a gloomy silence, an empty place of nightmares. For me, it was the liberation of darkness, a peaceful melody of chaos, where the ugliness would rise freely. The masks people wore during the day disappeared to expose their true monstrous faces. There was no more pretending. No more semblance of humanity.

I arrived at the manor, cloaked with its obscurity despite the moonlight shimmering. Wrenching the front door of my sanctuary open, I didn't meet my welcoming darkness nor the icy draft of the phantoms trying to escape this cursed place. Instead, a path of light lit up the hallway.

I took in the visible trail Lily had left displaying each of the activities she did before. Leaves were on the stairs—she had been by the greenhouse. I inched closer, following the path of light which led to the living room. The fire in the chimney was dying, but I could still hear its crackle. She had spent the night here.

And inside my living room was exactly where I found that flower goddess, asleep on my leather couch, wrapped around a blanket. There was a torn flower inside her hand. I observed every inch of her, from her peaceful breathing to her angelic features.

Her phone was unlocked on the table, still on the last page she was consulting on the web. Scientific reports about scents and perfume. A snarl twisted my face. She truly was her own kind of crazy.

I sat in front of her on my armchair and contemplated the warmth of the fire illuminating her face in an orange-and-sapphire color. Her lips parted, and that gesture alone made me jealous of the air she was sucking in and out. Even in the dark, she shone, reflecting her golden soul in this wretched world.

I was the monster watching the beautiful creature.

The beast taking in the beauty.

Evilness corrupting her dreams.

I didn't know for how long, perhaps minutes, perhaps hours, I stayed seated, unable to take my eyes off her nor move.

It was peaceful.

Satisfying even.

Lily slowly awoke, her nostrils flaring as if she could smell me in her dreams. She peeled her eyelids open and searched around her, probably wondering where the hell she was. When her tired eyes settled on mine, she adjusted herself, sitting up on the sofa.

"What time is it?" she asked with a shy smile.

"Five a.m."

A lucky guess, since my eyes refused to let go of her for a split second.

"I couldn't sleep." She pulled the blanket away from her, displaying her naked legs. "The manor is too big."

A jolt of garnet-red lust made my dick pulse greedily behind my zipper. My eyes captured her legs, most especially her thighs, before it traveled to her pointed nipples under her pink nightgown. It sent a fatal lick of poison to my dick, and a frustrated knot settled in my throat.

It was a miracle I somehow managed to reply, "Big?"

Like the fucking bulge you're making inside my pants.

"Yeah, I didn't want to sleep alone in the dark. That's why I came downstairs—I was waiting for you." She yawned, cuddling with herself by bringing her knees to her breasts.

A choice I was thankful for. Otherwise, the need to expose her naked breasts and lick, suck, claim her nipples would have run riot through me like hellions.

"You shouldn't have waited for me." Because if I knew she was, I wouldn't have been able to focus on idiots, knowing I could have claimed her over and over again.

"It's okay, I came to think about something anyway."

My gaze slithered to the shoulder strap of her nightgown that had dropped below her shoulder. It was torture. More blood rushed to my dick, the desire to kiss her neck scattering lava throughout my body.

"Enlighten me." A smile slanted my mouth, whilst my erection grew harder at the sight of her sultry lips and ponytail. *Devil's.* She'd be the end of me, and she knew it. I couldn't let my urges get the best of me. I wasn't that weak.

"You remember when I told you I wanted to be your equal," she mused, hesitant and sweet.

I nodded.

"Well, I'd like to be part of your world." She gulped and sat straighter on the couch, like a goddess about to make a regal speech. "I mean, I don't even know what you're truly doing for a job. Something with rocks?"

"I own luxury jewelry stores and mines, yes."

"Okay. That's a start." It was her turn to nod before she pulled a strand of her hair falling from her ponytail behind her ear. A ponytail I very much wanted to fist. "I also know what your club is about… At least, I think I do, but I don't want to be left out."

"It's not a pretty place, Lily." I pulled out my card and rolled it between my fingers, a corrosive possessiveness traveling in my veins. "It's not for you."

"I don't care." She hit me with her fiery stare, finally feeding me that witchcraft of hers. "It's a part of you."

"You remember the last time you went there," I threatened between clenched teeth. No man would ever approach her again without facing my wrath and insanity.

"They'll know I'm with you, won't they? So, it won't be like last time." Look at her. She was playing a game, gaining the assurance of the goddess that she was, and that made my dick pulse harder.

I always thought I'd rule alone, but maybe all kings needed a queen.

I denied the inevitable, and so did she.

Only she could match my darkness. If only I could get her fully to my side, tutoring her into accepting everything of hers. She was meant to rule hell with a crown of flowers on a throne of skulls.

It was about time to show them that Lily was mine.

This could be the perfect opportunity.

"As you said, there is no coming back from this," she added in a whisper, looking insecure now. In a flash, she erased that expression on her face, pulling her chin up.

"You'll have to obey my rules there, flower goddess," I snarled. "Can you obey me?"

"Yes." Her word was a lie, and her stare spoke the truth.

She was hellishly stubborn. She wouldn't obey me, and I wouldn't have it any other way. Punition was a price I'd like to inflict on her.

"Then spread your legs." I was aching for her.

She parted her legs, breathing deep. I was testing her, a question haunting my mind. How far was she willing to go inside her darkness? The card said death was awaiting. But perhaps I was reading it wrong.

The Lily everyone knew would die.

But she'd be reborn.

Not just like a flower goddess but the queen of hell.

She just didn't know it yet.

"I want your G-string gone," I ordered, desire burning my eyes to the point tears of blood would scatter to take my sight—and I'd blindly offer it to her if she demanded it.

She took her excuse of a panty off and dropped it on the floor. Her heartbeats stopped. Her pussy was bare. With a bite of her, she stayed silent, but I felt her body shot with static electricity. She unleashed the worst of me, my darkest compulsions resurrecting from the dead.

"Now, I'm gonna eat you." I lifted myself up from my seat and loomed toward her, readjusting my cuffs. "And tomorrow, the underworld will know you're mine."

Chapter 10

Lily

I had to make a choice.

Two dresses, both equally magnificent, were facing me on a hanger above the shelf. Both were the epitome of haute couture and royalty but were complete opposites.

A refined card was left among them, beautifully written, probably with a feather. Its inky smell of walnut notes, wet-sweet oakmoss, smoky leather, and black amongst the vetiver had filled my nostrils, sending me to a place of old, dusty books in a fairy-tale library.

Thunder unleashed on nature, its merciless lightning tinting the roaring sky in a gray-blue moonlight. The branches hit the glass like a fallen soul knocking on the window of my bedroom to find refuge inside the manor and escape the obscure air.

I spoke the words written on the card out loud between two lightning bolts.

As who will you come by my side?

Another growl from the sky, this one like a hungry monster awakening from the abyss of hell, raised the hair on my skin. It wasn't a simple dress to choose, no. This one would define my destiny just as one chooses a wedding dress. I buried my nails inside my palms, clamping them into tender flesh as I tried to think.

It was a devious test from Radcliff.

The first dress was as sweet as pink roses, smelling of the beauty of a ballet and a swan and of every princess's dream. It was elegant with an ivory corset. The sleeves fell below the shoulders and were transparent like a veil. It sparkled, as if one had taken all the stars of the universe to put them on this dress. Some flowers were sewn in rose-gold lace on the waist to form the most beautiful garden. It was my kind of perfection, and Radcliff knew it.

The other was from a pitch-black, starless sky, smelling of a royal court of night with a throne of bones and thorns. My heartbeat increased at the sight of it. This one screamed of power. The full-skirted dress was strapless with a plunging neckline formed of black roses, the edge of which burned into a flaming burgundy. It was more revealing than anything I'd ever owned. The bouffant skirt had different layers of satin. Crimson flowers were sewn down the length of it, like lianas rising from the bottom up.

Those were the two handmade dresses Radcliff had asked to be made for me.

Two sides of me.

Two futures I'd have to choose from.

Chapter 11

Lily

"Regretting your choice?" Radcliff's whisper warmed my nape, sending chills to my core.

The hellish front doors opened, and the air of corruption and madness enveloped me. Only one foot inside Club 7 and the heavy weight of the stares of the guests hidden behind their masks had fallen on us. The Devil and I, walking side by side, were the highlight of the spectacle, the twist that no one expected.

Radcliff had wrapped a possessive arm around my waist, gentle yet firm, as he guided me through the crowd, who had stopped their activities. I nestled in his darkness, and we leaped above the music and the show. Everything else apart from us became a blur.

The click-clack of my high heels echoed on the floor like a

murderous drum. I lifted my head, puffing my confidence into the aura surrounding me. *I won't regret my choice.* The sound of my shallow breath was the only symphony I could hear, like a time bomb clouding my thoughts.

In the red light of the club, the dark roses on my dress seemed to have taken on another form of life. They burned with hellfire, like the one that rose after the end of a battle after having inflicted chaos and destruction. As I passed in front of my reflection, the obsidian rocks on my flower tiara glittered like powerful stones needed for a ritual. My stare became a murder weapon, and my lace mask inked under my skin like a poison corrupting my cells.

The air had taken on the smell of green envy. By choosing the black dress, I was the flower with thorns ready to hail hell and gather its hellions. Radcliff's arm tightened around me, his hold taking root in me as if our souls had signed a bloody deal with a chalice. His touch sent a powerful electric shock on my skin, the kind that would leap flames of lust inside me. Tonight, he wouldn't leave my side, and at that moment, I knew I had made the right choice.

"Not one bit," I replied, boring my eyes into his, despite the black mask he wore. "Did I make the right choice?"

"There is no such thing as right or wrong." He shifted his head slowly toward me, a sinister snarl slipping free. "You've made the choice that your soul seeks."

"What about your soul?" I teased, convinced that by searching for his light, I had fallen into my darkness voluntarily, and worse, I wasn't ready to give it up. It was a dangerous game, where only one side could win. One of us could rise at the cost of destroying the other.

"I don't recall having one," he dropped with all his regal confidence, wetting his lip with a growing appetite. "But you certainly made your point, and you've compelled my black heart, spellbinding it with sins and more blackness than it had before, little witch."

All the air across my lungs vanished as if Radcliff had stolen the oxygen from the room and stopped time. I was his—it was a statement. A royal coronation. The weight of all the staring guests was nothing against the shadows of his calla lily eyes roaming my face, expressing the torment I was inflicting on him. Lust was like smoke encircling us, intoxicating us until we gave in.

We broke the eye contact—probably for my own good—and Radcliff gunned his eyes at the curious guests. Mostly men, the kind I wouldn't stay alone with in a dark hallway. They bowed their faces to the ground in an immediate reply, their fear of Radcliff stronger than their carnal impulses.

I chuckled, amused. "And you're proving yours."

"I don't need to prove that you're mine. They know." His Adam's apple bobbed, his scorching stare studying the crowd as if he wanted to keep the memory of this moment intact. "Their thoughts about you. I can feel them creeping through my scars. They'll pay."

"You can't condemn desire. It's human."

"My guests aren't humans. They're perverted monsters hiding behind masks." His grip tightened on me in a way that made me feel like he had taken me into a den with hungry lions. "They won't stop until they've hurt you. They want your tears and cries, not your pleasure."

A smile slanted his mouth into something twisted and Machiavellian. "They can watch you all they want. And they should. But it could also be the last damn thing they enjoy doing if they cross the line."

That warning should have sent a shiver down my spine, but it didn't. If anything, it sent a bolt of hot steam inside my belly. My gaze stumbled over the crowd, all those men who had done evil things or were the slaves to their perversions, with enough power to escape justice. They believed themselves untouchable, and for a moment, an impulse took seed in me: I wanted to stir up their

gaze, their desire, so the Devil would exercise his wrath and darkness. I wanted them to pay for what they would have done to me
that night at the club.

Only the bigger monster could beat the others. Radcliff was
mocking them. Owning them by taking advantage of their weak-
nesses, and that... aroused me.

No. I snapped the thought out of my head, promising myself I
wouldn't nourish that lethal seed planted in me. I couldn't think that.
I would never want Radcliff to inflict chaos. I chose goodness and
faith, and I was dancing with the blackness only to deliver Radcliff's
soul from the monster chaining it.

This seed was seeking to poison the other cells in my body,
when my gaze crossed Hugo's. He gasped at the sight of the couple
that we formed, with his jaw open. It was hard to tell who he was
most surprised by: Radcliff ruling over the shadows with someone,
or me, arm in arm with the Devil. He then grinned in approbation
and saluted me with a nod.

I smiled back coyly at Hugo, as if we shared a secret no one else
knew. Radcliff didn't even notice him, stepping to the stairs leading to his office. He held out his hand for me to follow him, but my
gaze shifted to Melissa.

She was in the opposite corner to us, her elbow attached to a
broom. She wore a wide orange jumpsuit with high heels, a messy
ponytail, and cleaning gloves. Why was she doing this? Nothing of
that looked like her. She sent me the most evil of looks, one that
screamed of jealousy and hatred, and a bad feeling crept under my
spine.

"Let's go," Radcliff said stiffly, a muscle contracting in his jaw,
still waiting for me to seize his hand.

I let him take me into the dark for a couple of seconds until the
door of his office cracked open. Dim candles lit up his desk, from

which a man was standing backward, holding a loupe, inspecting whatever was on the table.

The man faced us at the sound of Radcliff's footsteps approaching on the parquet, a smile hanging on his thin lips. He was probably the same age as my uncle, with gray hair and a badly shaved beard. "Mr. Radcliff, I did as you requested."

"Lily, this is the man we call LaMouette. A diamond expert." Radcliff introduced us with a gesture of his hand while getting rid of his mask as he strolled to his desk. "LaMouette, this is *my* Lily."

I followed him and pulled my mask away, nodding politely. "It's nice to meet you."

LaMouette gave me a slight nod, probably not daring to keep his attention on me for too long next to Radcliff. He smelled of sea notes and seaweed. My breathing increased. It was the first time Radcliff was introducing me to his world—and to other people apart from Hugo. I didn't want to screw up or let them believe I was just a child that couldn't match the charisma that inhabited him.

I approached the desk, where diamonds were exposed on a burgundy satin sheet. Radcliff took something that looked like tweezers to grab a diamond and brought the loupe to his eyes, inspecting every inch of it with the same devotion he showed when we were having sex. The way his gaze had the power to strip you naked, making you feel like the most treasured being in the world. I swallowed the fact it turned me on.

"Do you know how to choose a diamond?" Radcliff asked me without shifting his hard and focused stare from it.

"No, I don't." My breath cut short. If that was Radcliff's test, I was definitely not doing well.

"You need to take into account the 4 C's. Carat. Cut. Color. Clarity." He dropped the loupe, his stare focusing on mine in a way that made my stomach boil. "Do you believe in magic, Lily?"

"Yes," I breathed.

Something about Radcliff infused dark magic and enchantment. "There have been stories for centuries around diamonds. It's commonly said that gemstones grow from pain in hell and have remarkable properties," he continued, turning every facet of the stone between his fingers. "But diamonds hold a symbolism of wealth, power, and even the promise of a happily ever after. Marriage."

At the word "marriage," Radcliff had eclipsed everything else but him, and the smell of dahlias and anemones captured my nose. A crimson blush tinted my cheeks, the flames of the candles melting me. He tilted his lips into a thin line. The kind that replaced the dahlias with black roses and the anemones with chrysanthemum. The kind that had deliberately wanted to stir that reaction in me.

"Diamonds are diamonds because of their rarity. They represent the human desire to rise above their condition. They can reflect all sorts of colors, just like human emotions. They can even defy the dark by glowing despite the surrounding chaos—"

I listened, captivated. Not by diamonds, but by Radcliff's passion in his discourse. It accelerated my heart. Coiled my belly. Bloomed my cells. For me, flowers had souls and were my friends. For him, gemstones had properties. We weren't that different after all. We'd just chosen a different path.

"Are diamonds your favorite precious stone?" I cut him off in a burst of speech as if I couldn't hold on to the words or they'd have burnt my tongue.

His eyes sparkled with amusement and secrets that wedged into the depths. "Discovered, yes."

"Discovered?" My lips parted.

LaMouette smiled in a way the answer seemed evident to him, and Radcliff's expression remained like unyielding marble.

"Pick one." Radcliff changed the subject, referring to the diamonds. "Which one is speaking to you?"

I obeyed the weight of his stare falling upon me and focused, my gaze slithering on the diamonds. I was directly drawn to one small diamond shaped like a heart. It was hidden in the back, probably because of its imperfection—half-broken inside with small breaks, it was nonetheless beautiful, glittering like fairy dust. In every shade of pink, from light to dark, it reflected the light as much as it held the darkness, and I could imagine the tale that it once upon a time belonged to a princess before it got itself bewitched by a witch.

"This one." I indicated the precious gem with my finger.

LaMouette reached for it with his transparent gloves before giving it to me. I let the small diamond fall inside my palms, holding it carefully as if it were a fragile beating heart—in a way, it felt like having the key to Radcliff's iron heart.

"Then, this is yours," Radcliff stated, and my eyes widened on him.

"What jewel would you like to be made with it?" LaMouette asked. "Necklace, bracelet, ring?"

"I'm not sure I—" I entrapped the heart into my palm, a smile curving my lips under their perplexed stares. "Something that doesn't alter the stone. I want to wear it this way. It's perfect in its own way. Honest, just as it is."

Radcliff's gaze traveled to the diamond I was clutching close to my heart. "LaMouette, you can leave now."

The diamond expert gathered the other diamonds, taking care to pack them away carefully, and neither Radcliff nor I unhooked our gazes from each other. The air between us swiveled into a macabre dance, which would resuscitate all the skeletons of the neighboring cemeteries.

"It fits you well," Radcliff dropped, referring to the gemstone, his low voice edging with forbidden desire.

"Because it's flawed and imperfect," I sighed, enclosing my diamond inside the small dark velvet box LaMouette had posed on the desk.

LaMouette grabbed the box, nodding at us one last time before slipping out of the room, and the tension between Radcliff and me exploded freely.

"No," Radcliff corrected, eyebrows pinching together. "As you said before, it's perfect in its own way. It's reflecting light with a potential for darkness. Beautiful and…" A hint of a smile lifted his lips, while with the tips of his fingers, he extinguished the flame of a candle, which turned to smoke. "Complicated, despite that pink-heart *princess* facade. One that many can't understand its true nature and wants."

But he could. He could speak to my soul in a language of his own. My finger brushed the length of the table, my teeth tugging on my lower lip. "And which gemstone would you be if I'm the pink diamond?"

"The rock. Probably the coal or the iron." He blew out another candle so that only the dim light of a lamp remained.

The smoke curled out in the room like a velvet-clad cloak of dark omens, smelling of a pantomime of devilry and prayers inside a cathedral. Chills spread. He did it on purpose. By blowing out the candle, he had sprayed the scent of the oil, and he knew it'd magnetize my nose, leading me to the imaginary kingdom of his choice.

I ventured across his office, the refined shades of black drawing me closer to his world. "I disagree with you. I may not know about rocks, but I do know about perfume and—" I inhaled the murky scent of coal, amber, and tuberose. "You're no coal nor iron."

Radcliff loomed in my direction. I could feel his presence following me like a shadow watching over me as I gazed out of the enormous window. I peered at the depravation inside his club of elite guests, my breath misting the glass.

"If diamonds were to be a perfume," I started, closing my eyes, "it'd be a base note of wood smoke from the way they're born from a chunk of coal. They are molded by the darkness and burned to grow, so I'd add an amber and vanilla scent. Brought to hell through a volcanic eruption, the smell of tobacco and sandalwood would fit perfectly coupled with the softness of a rose in a message of hope for the hardest stone on earth."

"Your point." His voice was like poppy tears sending me into a dreamlike and hypnotic state.

I slammed my eyes open, encountering Radcliff's reflection on the window from behind me. Only darkness accompanied him, trying to engulf him into the void. But he emerged from the dark like a fallen god.

"Don't you see?" I smiled. "You're the diamond in the rough."

Chapter 12

Radcliff

Lily was playing with hellfire.

She had worn the black onyx dress and had, in doing so, chosen her side. She had played my game, and as a consequence, everything about her was a constant frustrating temptation. My dick hardened just at the sight of that flower goddess swimming in my element. Thirsty for every unholy thing with her.

Her fingers delicately grazed my window glass, her naked back exposed to me. I was ripping the infernal crimson flowers and the black fabric apart with my eyes, hoping the tissue could melt into ashes. It was a torture I'd inflict on myself over and over again. I cracked my knuckles, my urges washing over me like a hot tide. An unbreakable spell.

Lily then made the wrong choice of peering upon the cameras in my club. Horror consumed her eyes at the view of what was happening inside the dungeons—orgies and fetishism. She backed off from it like it was a toxic smell to her. Her face was ashen, and she swallowed her questions away, attempting to maintain a cool expression.

"You shouldn't watch that." I tensed, approaching her.

She faced me, her heartbeat leaping in her throat. "Do you?" She paused. "Do you enjoy that?"

I had better things to do than watch them. If nothing else, all of them were despicable to me and inspired only repulsion. All of that creation was for a bigger purpose than desire. Club 7 was a matter of personal revenge.

"I'll take pleasure in everything with you." That was the truth. She was my sin, and she had to pay the consequences for having awakened the worst of my remaining mortality. One that sought domination, possession and had a constant hunger. "I'll never share you—you're mine—but…" I towered over her, an arm on the window next to her head. "If I would have to lay eyes upon them, it'd be to punish them after they've watched me possessing you."

"I thought you never liked an audience." Her voice was edged with excitement and fear.

I brushed my mouth to her nape. "Not when they'll worship what is mine, but for now…"

Her lips parted, and the bulge inside my pants kept on pulsing like a horny teenager. I needed to have her. Right now. In one move, I switched the cameras to the entrance and main area, silencing their shows inside the red rooms, only to notice that my new guest had arrived.

Carmin Junior.

A snarl twisted my mouth at the view of Junior making his way through my guests. He looked like a lost duck, his eyes swiveling to every corner of my club. The little prince was about to taste the fruit of my revenge.

Lily brushed her fingers on my torso, and that was enough to make me lose my self-control. I pinned her against the window, my lips crashing savagely into hers. I gripped her waist in a way she wouldn't escape me. The sweet noise of her moans made me cup her jaw. I needed to feel her soul. Tongues intertwined. I was a starving beast, and she was the unfortunate holder of my charcoal dusty humanity.

I needed more.

More of her.

The violence of the way she bit and sucked on my lip made my veins boil. Taking control of the kiss, I consumed her until I stole all of her breaths and inked my blackness inside her. I wanted her insanity. Her darkness. Her everything.

"Radcliff…"

I didn't let her finish, making her spin and collide on my desk. My hardness pressing on her belly, I clenched the desk with my fists on each side of her, my tensing muscles trapping her. Our gazes locked with animalistic breathing and dilated pupils.

"You have three seconds to back away." *One…* If she didn't back off, I wouldn't be the master of myself any longer. *Two…* She didn't pull away, wetting her lower lip instead. *Three…* She had sealed her fate.

"Get down on your knees, flower goddess," I ordered with a sinister expression.

Her eyes held mine, and for a moment, I thought she'd retract. She then shifted position for me to lean against the desk and for her to face me. I pressed the button giving me access to the windows as her lips parted, her eyes roaming my face one last time before she went down on her knees.

Christ. I felt my Adam's apple bobbing. The breathing of the monster in me intensified at the idea of being satiated and dominating the apple of his obsession by submitting her to her knees. Her fingers stroked my aching hardness, and a muscle in my jaw tightened.

"Show me you're mine." My fingers tangled in her hair, magnetized by her angel face about to do something so devilish.

She opened the zipper of my pants and freed my erection. She approached me, angling her head so she'd lick my whole length. My head fell backward, and blood hissed like lava through each of my cells. It was like a shot of adrenaline.

"Fuck, don't stop." I contracted my grip on the desk with a groan when she took me whole inside her sultry lips.

I pulsed inside her mouth, and she met my drives, slow at first, sucking me with all her goddesship. I fisted her hair, and her eyes locked on mine from below. Just that view would make me jerk off.

"Harder." The starving beast in me groaned.

In and out, her lips were a paradise meant to torture gods. She sucked and licked my length faster, both of her hands gripping my torso. It took all the strength in the goddamn universe to not drive her mouth further on my cock and pound into her with all my madness.

Lily took the initiative to tease my tip with her tongue, and I cursed. A new wave of possessiveness lashed into me like a deadly scourge. Where the hell did she learn that?

"Did you do that before?" I ascended into a murderous falsetto. *Do I need to unalive the bastard who had the unworthy privilege to be your first?*

"No." She teased my tip again with her temptress's tongue, pride shining through the amber of her eyes. "Am I any good?"

"Sinfully good." My lips twisted, and I became hell. My inner demons couldn't be stopped anymore.

I thrust inside her mouth with all the fire she ignited in me. I was a madman. I could feel my scar burning, reopening, and my eyes reddening with hunger. The monster in me was being fed, the ugliness of my being coming to life.

She slowed down her pace, and inside my inferno, I came across my horrified guest through the glass, standing on the stairs leading to my office. Junior was staring with narrowed eyes at the window, his face as pale as a ghost. I had pushed the button to change my one-way window to a see-through window. It wasn't completely what I had in mind when I had sent him an invitation to meet after his constant whining, but that would do. I was supposed to scare him away with facts and show in a gracious way that Lily was mine only. But fuck the gracious way—brutally tasted so good. I should have felt like a bastard, but I was only possessed by revenge.

She was mine.

Lily worked her sweet mouth across my length, and I fought every urge to come. Carmin Junior kept watching Lily from the back sucking me and taking pleasure in it. My eyes sent flames of rage at him, and a sardonic smile curled my lips. *That's the endgame for you and your daddy.* He could go back to jerking off like a teenager.

I thought he would cry, his mouth curving with disgust. He was pitiful, with eyebrows slanting inward and eyes wetting. I caressed Lily's hair, my jaw tensing. The message had been sent.

The moment he left, running away, I switched the windows back to one-way. I had no desire to show anyone what would happen next. I made Lily stand up and felt the need to kiss her, perhaps as forgiveness or as a reminder she'd never escape me.

"I want you, little witch," I cursed.

"To what point?" she teased, her eyes shining with her witchcraft.

"The most terrible part of hell."

I unfastened her corset, dropped her dress to the floor. The lights in my office flickered, their color impregnating the passionate red of our demons chanting together. I turned her over, making her naked chest collide against the cold glass.

She gasped, her two palms sticking on the window. "Is that your worst?"

I slapped her ass, making her jump and moan against the glass again. I pulled her thong up, and her back arched in reply, her butt caressing my cock.

"Silence, flower goddess, or else I'll have to shut you up with these panties of yours. Or worse, I'll stop." I would not stop. I couldn't. I was too deep in my desire for her to back away.

She nodded, and I slapped her other ass cheek. The sound of my hand clapping into her made a red jolt of lust head straight to my cock. Her cheek collided with the window, and I ran my hand between her legs, feeling how wet my little witch was.

"You're so fucking wet. Is this turning you on?" I grabbed her pussy, and that moan of hers was so delicious. "Do you want me to slap your pussy too?"

Her cheek reddened in a way I had guessed a secret she didn't wish to share—as if she could hide anything from me. I *knew* what was inside her soul.

"I want you to say it," I murmured. "After all, you've been bad today. You sucked your first"—*and last*—"cock."

She parted her legs in reply, her wetness pooling over my hand as I caressed her through her panties. I licked my lips, the desire to taste her juices and drive inside of her stronger than anything.

"Yes, I want you to," she gasped. "Please."

I pulled aside her panties, and she clenched her hip forward to feel my touch. My dick was agonizing with all this teasing. I gave a little slap on her pussy, and she threw her head back, biting her lip to keep her from screaming. She rolled her hips again, demanding more punishment, her juices spreading on my window. I gave another slap to her clit. And again. She tucked her stomach in, her legs shaking as a smile spread across her face.

Her regal darkness matched mine.

I switched aside to get a better view of her butt from above, and I pulled away the strands of hair hiding her beautiful face. I took off my tie and smacked her butt cheek with it. Her hot breath created a cloud of mist, and when her angelic eyes fell upon my devil ones with a vivid glow, I did it again. Only I could bring that delicious wickedness inside of her. Only I could corrupt the light in her. Only with her, I became human.

"You're so gorgeous," I admitted in my agony. I couldn't wait anymore.

The moment I slammed into her, it seemed that a torrent of lava had dragged me with it in its fall. I was no longer a master of anything. My mouth lingered on her nape, overdoing it like a thirsty vampire. The room was a sauna, ripping my scars apart and tearing my skin.

Her butt against my cock made me drive harder inside her. She pressed her cheek against the window harder, and I gripped her waist on each side to hold back my monstrous urges. Her heartbeat pounded in her throat, her eyebrows slanting inward in pleasure. My ugliness adored her the only way it knew how to, mercilessly and possessively.

She bent further, the trace of her fingers descending on the glass. I thrust inside her in all my brutality, keeping her at my mercy. I yielded to taking everything from her. For her soul and heart to be exclusively mine. For every inch of her goddess body to be mine to cherish, consume, and abuse.

"Radcliff, I—" she moaned, her legs shaking and her strength vanishing from her.

I hooked an arm around her and brought her to my desk. She sat on it and wrapped her legs around my hips instinctively as if she, too, could read my primal thoughts. Our lips sealed in a kiss that drew me to her by an invisible force. Perhaps darkness had bound us together.

I grabbed her breast with my palm and lowered my mouth to it, sucking, licking, and nibbling on her nipple. She craned her neck with pleasure while I worshipped her the way she should be.

I retracted with a pinch on her nipple and gave it a light slap. She lay down on her back, and she raised her arms to grab the end of the desk behind her, offering me a sumptuous view of all of her beauty, from her perfectly rounded breasts to the curves of her hips. Her cheeks were crimson—as red as her ass cheeks—contrasting with that golden skin of hers. My breath was ragged. I felt my heart darkening even more, each of my scars burning under my skin.

Entering her sacred walls again, I put her legs on my shoulders and kissed her ankles. I hit the end of her, slow but deep, until I was sure she'd feel me in her stomach. Her grip tightened on the desk, her back arching.

I increased my pace, and she spread her legs wider, dropping them a bit below my shoulders. That view was enough to unleash my hell. My thumb on her clit, I locked eyes with that goddess, driving my merciless thrusts deeper, faster, harder inside her. My other hand kept her in place as she sucked in her stomach, her breathing heaving.

She released her hands from the desk to cover mine, digging her fingers into my grip. Her brows slanted inward until her orgasm consumed her whole, to the point that she tried to push me away from inside her.

A bolt of fire ignited me as I watched her surrender to her impulses in all her beauty. I broke against her wave, hitting deep inside her one last time, my orgasm crashing brutally with a low growl.

I hit the desk with my palms, towering on top of her. My breathing was animalistic and beastly, as if I had hunted my prey for long hours. Drops of sweat slid down my forehead. I was a bloodred-eyed monster, and she was the fallen goddess. She grazed her fingers from my biceps to my torso, not keeping her sunny eyes that set me aflame away from me.

She smiled then, one that was half-sweet and loving. The gracious one she'd give when she was talking about perfume.

But it also twitched with something else. Something malicious, sharp, and dark.

The Tower. The Death. The cards were against us from the start. They'd warned me, but now I couldn't escape our destiny written by bloody stars.

Fate had predicted she'd be the queen to my hell.

But the prophet also had said that love would deliver me.

I never wanted to be saved.

So which fate will you choose, Lily?

My queen or my tragic ending.

Darkness or light.

Chapter 13

Lily

My hand brushed against the glass serving as a shield between my creations and the rest of the world.

The red smoke inside the aphrodisiac swiveled across the tube. In the shade, both it and my perfume were a haze of purple breath like forbidden magical elixirs.

The longer I let it macerate, the more the properties of the Devil's Corpse engulfed the other liquids. The hellish particles similar to a burning fire danced in the vial like fairy dust.

It would only take a drop of pure desire to change humanity forever.

The perfume was magnificent, like a heavenly potion of love. A powerful aroma of the most sophisticated scents. With every shade of pink and purple, it was a masterpiece holding the fantasy of dreams and the power of human passion.

The aphrodisiac was hellbound, a destructive weapon that would submit humanity to its most hidden sins and desires.

I caught sight of my reflection in the glass. My eyes had darkened, contrasting with my rose flower headband. I wore a corset in a bewitching color, halfway between the pink rose and the queen of the night tulip, on top of a white spring dress—with sheer sleeves and fabric so light, this outfit would inspire romance and purity.

I was just as contradictory as my inventions—the perfume was from heaven, the aphrodisiac bound in hell, and I was stuck on a path in between. I was becoming one with the shadows, and the more I stayed inside the cold realm of Radcliff, the more I was losing perspective of my actions.

I needed to win the soul of the Devil in order to make him see the light—but instead, I was enjoying the power of the darkness, the thrill of being by Radcliff's side, and the freedom to explore who I was without filter.

My gaze drifted from the spell of the perfume, and I exited the lab, ambling through the fresh breeze and the calm of the morning. Even the harsh, raucous call of the ravens was a safe haven to my soul. I entered the greenhouse with only one certitude. Only time would tell which one of our downfalls it would be. Which kingdom would expand. Which one of us would triumph.

I inhaled the odors of the blooming flowers standing like a royal court. I sat below the Devil's Corpse, feeling the need to hang out with her.

"It's my birthday today," I confessed with a smile, celebrating my twenty-second birthday alone with the flowers.

"My mom would be proud of me." I played nervously with

my dress, the intoxicating scents wafting up my nostrils in shades of happiness. "I just wished she was here to see what I've accomplished."

Since she died, I'd never truly celebrated my birthday. I had no reason to. I wasn't one to celebrate with friends, nor had any of them, apart from Adonis and Uncle. Adonis was usually busy on business with his father, as for Uncle, he simply forgot. Plus, I hadn't achieved anything worthy. It was just a lost year for me. But this year was different. I had a reason to celebrate, and for once, I craved someone to make this day special. To make me feel special.

"This is stupid," I snorted. "It's like, you always want what you don't have?" *Love.*

My phone vibrated in the pocket of my dress, as if the ghosts had delivered me a message. It was a text from my uncle, or more precisely a GIF of a cat holding a present, "Happy Birthday" written in glittery colors underneath.

At least he's trying. I replied with a thank-you and posed my phone on the stone. I jumped abruptly when I heard the motor of a car. The gate was closed; it was coming from the manor. Someone was leaving.

"I need to go." I rushed to the exit, my heart hammering.

The noise of the screaming engine was from an old-fashioned black car parked in front of the manor. It looked like one of those luxurious cars from the forties. Next to it, Mr. Walton was going back and forth with some luggage. Radcliff was leaving. At the thought, panic rushed to my veins. I would be alone once more. I swallowed my feelings and continued my way through the entrance with fast steps.

Radcliff appeared in front of the main door, adjusting his five-piece tailored suit. Refined and elegant in his usual black, he was definitely going somewhere. He crossed his arms on his chest, his stare hitting me with questioning. He smelled the scent of the candle blown on a birthday, the one you make a wish with.

"You're going somewhere?" I asked, the pounding of my heart thumping widely like a fleeing horse.

"Yes." Radcliff passed next to me, and my heart seemed to buzz in my ears. He inspected his car with a deadly stillness before focusing his attention back on me. "So are you."

My mind thought of a hundred possibilities. The main one included that he had gotten tired of me and that this was my ride back. I dug my fingers into the flesh of my palms.

"Where?" I squared my shoulders, trying to mask my feelings.

"We're going to Grasse."

My mouth opened. My eyes widened. "Really?"

Radcliff's lips twisted into a snarl.

Grasse. We're going to Grasse. A bolt of excitement ran through me, and all the scents around me had seemed to burst into a festival of fireworks.

Radcliff readjusted his cufflinks, which shone like diamonds. "It's your birthday, if I recall?" *He knew.* He then opened the passenger door with that cold-blooded grace of his. "We're leaving now. Your bags are already packed."

I didn't move, still shocked that Radcliff had planned this trip for me. I didn't bother to ask him how he knew about my birthday—after all, Radcliff knew everyone's secrets.

"You remembered." I was breathless.

He had remembered the talk we had that day on the cliff about my mother and about the place I dreamed of going to. It was the most wonderful surprise someone could ever do.

"Of course, I did." He gave me his hand so I, the witch, would step inside her carriage.

There was no word I could possibly speak to describe how I

felt. I shot a last glance in the direction of the greenhouse, a part of me wanting to share my happiness with the Devil's Corpse. I wanted to tell her that I was wrong. Someone was here.

"I don't even know when your birthday is." I smiled at the man who could read my soul. The one whose secrets remained to be unfolded.

"And you don't have to. My birth isn't worth celebrating; that's why I never gave it any importance. Yours, on the contrary, is a different matter." He invited me once again to grab his hand in his gentlemanly manner.

"I disagree." My smile deepened. "One day, you'll tell me. You'll see. I'll make you change your mind."

His lips curled into a thin line. "I wouldn't bet on it, flower goddess."

I seized Radcliff's hand and stepped inside the Devil's car. And soon, we'd be on our way to my heaven.

The fields of flowers were never-ending.

I'd stepped inside a sugary world, a rich spectacle of rainbows of colors, from sweet pink to crystal white and purple love. Radcliff's private plane had landed, wafting on the flowers like a heavy breeze. Flying in luxury had been a new experience for me, but this scenery was like nothing I'd seen before.

I stepped outside the plane, rushing to the fields like it was my oxygen. A need. The floral scents tingled my nostrils—creamy tuberose, bright peony, purple-hazed lavender, magnificent jasmine, and roses—and a smile took over my face. The sun was beaming on this paradise, and I had only one desire.

"It's wonderful." I took off my ballerina flats for my bare feet to touch the grass. I reeled around to peer at Radcliff behind me. "Can I?"

He nodded as if he knew this question was coming. I laughed and didn't wait for him to rush through the field. My hair swayed with the wind, the spring breeze bloomed my cells, and the grass on my bare legs was the touch of freedom and wildness. I passed my hands through the plants like one felt the need to hug.

I engulfed myself deeper in this paradise, becoming one with the flowers. I ran through them until the sun arrived on my back. I stopped at the view of the forest standing at the end of the path. It was the opposite to the one at Ravencliff Manor. This one was bright and welcoming, holding the power of white magic with birds singing the melody of love. A realm of scents, a kingdom where humans weren't allowed and where faeries ruled.

I turned around, finding Radcliff far away behind me. I waved at him, impatient for him to join me. But then, seeing him in the midst of the flowers, it tightened my heart and cut my breath short. My cells reacted, puffing up with a whole new feeling—something more powerful than lust and more destructive than an aphrodisiac.

I tried to ignore it, but the feeling inked through my core. The gleaming sun tinted the flowers in a golden undertone; its rays gilded the whole surroundings as an offering from the gods. They hit Radcliff's back, like a dark king braving the field of rose centifolia.

I had to glance away before my heart combusted. Next to the jasmine field, the sight of another field shot me with an electric shock.

"I can't believe there is a field of lilies of the valley here," I said breathlessly, hypnotized by their clusters of little white bells and glossy leaves. "This place is heaven."

I hopped in their direction, and a feeling of nostalgia rocked me. My mom would have loved this, her Lily in the middle of the lilies. I twirled around the flowers in a circle, and in the middle of one of my spins, the view of Radcliff under the shadow of a tree, leaning casually on the branch, made me stop. I blew out one of my locks of hair that had fallen over my eyes and returned his ghost of a smile with a full one.

"Seeing all of this is the best birthday gift I could ever receive." I bit my lower lip. "I can't thank you enough."

Radcliff grabbed a vibrant red apple from the tree that he examined before keeping it locked inside his palm. "What about owning them?"

"What?"

"You own those fields, Lily." A sardonic smile slipped free from his lips as he made the apple travel between his fingers.

"You can't buy flowers." I shook my head, not believing my nose that he had done that.

"You can when you're a flower queen or goddess." He finally stepped out from the shadow, dropping the apple on the ground. He hid the sun from us, towering over me with all his strength and mystery. "I said I'd burn the world to find you and spare only a field of flowers—"

"Because that's the only place you'll ever find me," I continued, feeling my breath being sucked out from my lungs. "Here."

He had given me not only a crown but a court of royal subjects.

"Those fields are yours." With one of his fingers, he grazed my skin, trailing a strand of my hair away from my face to tuck it behind my ear. Soft and possessive, that touch was a promise. "You can come here as much as you'd like. If what Delange told me is true, these fields are supposed to be the best in Grasse."

"I can't believe this."

I had broken the few inches separating us to throw myself against his hard body. I stood on my tiptoes and let his arms capture me, keeping me locked in with him, safe and secure. My lips met his with lust and need. The type of kiss that could open portals, where you're drinking the other's soul and never being satiated. The one that consumes you like the most enthralling of poison.

The Devil in his eyes plummeted me back to his dark, burning world. His pomegranate taste bound me with the damned. The seal of our lips was an unsaid contract written in blood. And yet, despite all of that, that kiss was beautiful and hopeful. One where you know where you belong.

The kiss disappeared into the past when I stumbled backward, hearing the sound of an animal passing through the foliage. My eyes darted to the forest, then to the fields, until stopping a few meters in front of us.

It was a doe.

Her ears were pulled back as her gaze shifted between us and the apple Radcliff had dropped on the grass. She bowed her head to it, not moving forward nor backward.

"She's not afraid," I whispered and crouched, advancing slowly in front of her.

Behind me, Radcliff remained immobile. Through the doe's eyes, I believed she could hold moments of the past like a crystal ball. Magic. Those same eyes were the color of the oldest tree, a symbol of wisdom and faith. They traveled back and forth to the apple once more, before she retreated one step.

I leaned toward the fruit and seized it inside my palm. The apple was a burning red color, apart from a slight part that had turned to a dark crimson color as if enchanted.

"This is what you want?" I held out the apple to her, stretching out my arm, but the doe's gaze was fixed on Radcliff.

I slowly turned my head behind me to see that Radcliff too had a firm gaze with the animal. Neither of them flinched. They locked eyes in a staring contest. Long seconds passed, and it felt like nature had stopped its course for both of them to communicate.

Life seemed to have started again when the doe walked slowly to him. She was still mistrustful, but she remained hypnotized by the man bound to hell. She passed in front of me, ignoring my presence.

"The apple," Radcliff commanded, his mouth not moving as if it was a thought he had conveyed to me.

I gave back the apple to Radcliff, being careful not to frighten the doe. He held it by the stem, and in response, the animal opened her nostrils to smell it, angling her head to bite the apple.

I sat on the grass, watching two opposites becoming attracted. "How are you doing that?"

"Purity craves the most of evil. Sins. It's all about balance. The yin and the yang." With a turn of his hand, the apple was now inside his palm. "Eat," he ordered the doe.

The doe bit the apple and seized it in her mouth before running back in the direction of the forest.

"Perhaps you're just good with animals." I rose up, raising an eyebrow at him. That doe had just made my point. "She didn't come to you because you're evil, but perhaps because her purity allowed her to see the true color of your heart."

A scowl slanted his lips. "Then she must be blind."

It was one of Radcliff's tricks, to hide the better part of his humanity behind the Devil's mask. But I wouldn't give up on him. Through the immensity of the trees inside the fairy forest, my eyes landed on the doe. She was still there, hiding between the branches, and this time, she had her gaze fixed on me.

"The view is not the most relatable of sense." I smiled. "The scent is—with intuition if you believe in the seven senses."

"You do have an answer for everything, little witch."

"Says the Devil," I quipped back, drifting my eyes back to him.

But something in the background distracted me. My eyebrows knitted inward when men in black costumes traveled back and forth with golf carts through my flower fields. Some of them held umbrellas and stayed rigid like royal guards.

"Who are they? What are they doing?" My tone was defensive.

"Your security." Radcliff sauntered past the landscape of blooms to head back to our ride. "They guard the fields against every type of intruder. Day and night."

"Really?"

Radcliff's stare hit mine, and I had my answer. Radcliff never joked.

"The doe can come if she wants. I don't want anything to happen to her," I added, running to catch him.

"You'll do as you please. It'll be your orders. I have no power over *your* fields."

The way he accentuated the word *your* bloomed my heart. The most magical land was mine.

"You think I should make a list just in case and give it to the guards?" I considered, lifting my head with pride. "I'll make a list," I decided with a smile, facing Radcliff's silence.

My stomach growled and rumbled loudly. Under all this excitement, I had forgotten to eat. "Where are we going now?"

"We'll stay somewhere private for the night." By that, he probably meant a villa far away from the city and luxurious enough for Radcliff's taste.

"I was wondering… perhaps we could grab a bite in the

city?" I asked hesitantly, my fingers intertwining together. "I'm starving, and it'd be nice to visit the center."

"I'm not going into the city." His tone didn't leave any room for argument.

His face closed up as the sunset behind him faded away through the valley. I hadn't said my last word yet. This time, I would be the one testing him. He drew me to the darkness; I'd do the same with the light.

"I understand. I'll just go alone, then. But I left my phone at the manor, so I won't be able to contact you." Not that I had his phone number. I sighed dramatically—if I had to play Radcliff's game, the only way to win was through his possessiveness. "I'll stay near the lights while walking through the night, and if I'm lost, I'll just ask someone to help me."

He didn't reply, but the way he fired his stare at me was answer enough.

I knew he wouldn't let me go alone.

Just like I knew I was the more stubborn of us.

Chapter 14

Lily

"You really had to close down the entire restaurant?" I asked, carrying the paper swan with the rest of my dish inside. "The poor owner couldn't even put two words together at the end."

Radcliff had paid to privatize the most exclusive restaurant in Grasse for us to dine alone with no other guests. The owner was reluctant at first, but it took the Devil only thirty seconds for him to change his mind and for us to eat as we pleased in the back of the restaurant like in a glamorous cave.

Radcliff's lips drew into a sinister line. "Just like you ordered three dishes."

I laughed as Radcliff and I continued our midnight walk around the center of Grasse. Together, we made the weirdest team. Me, ordering the dishes for an ogre, and the merciless king of hell for a client—whose discontentment would destroy the owner's career. The poor owner was sweating his guts out, afraid that something would go wrong. And as much as I hated to admit it, it was by far the funniest night I had lived.

"At least I finished two of those dishes." I showed Radcliff my swan, smelling the delicious odor of truffles. "And I'll finish the third later tonight."

Radcliff posed his hand behind my back at the view of a man passing in our dark alley. He was lit up under the streetlights, unlike us. The stranger's gaze swept over me with a longing smile that faded the moment his eyes rested on Radcliff.

Radcliff's hand behind my back tensed, and the stranger lowered his eyes to the ground, quickening his steps to get away from us as fast as possible to escape the Devil's merciless gaze. Even Radcliff's long black coat's shadow was frightening on the stones. It made him look supernatural. He could have passed for a dark magician with the hat he wore to probably hide his scar.

I barely saw his scar anymore. It was a part of him, what made him the Devil that aroused me and the phantom that understood me. But the look of the passengers and the workers at the restaurant had been fixed on it with terror. They made him their villain, and the thought of what Radcliff had to go through all these years cracked my heart.

When we stepped out of the narrow street, we arrived at the town center, a blinding light coming from a shop making us stop. Only one window wasn't closed off, illuminating the whole place.

It displayed the new advertising for Carmin's No. 27, the perfume that, despite everything, had remained my favorite. A masterpiece. In the picture, a young woman was wearing the fragrance, the world bowing at her feet. Surrounded by gilding, she was the queen of the universe.

I inched closer to the window. There was a huge picture of Christian displaying a wide, white smile, with a heart logo and text written below:

The legend, the great Carmin, was born here, building an empire of excellence in the perfumery world.

At least he isn't a megalomaniac. I swallowed, my stare stopping at an advertisement of Carmin's latest male perfume. Adonis was the model for their oceanic fragrance, standing on a yacht with two women almost making out with him. It was oversexualized, selling Adonis as a golden boy even though he was much more than that.

"One day, I'll have this," I murmured more to myself than to Radcliff, contemplating the boutique that was the epitome of luxury and success.

"Why settle for only that," Radcliff dropped, his gaze fixed on the smiling picture of Christian Carmin. His jaw knotted, and murder spread in his eyes like burning hellfire. "Carmin is no legend. He's barely an emperor, whose reign would be short."

Radcliff pulled his Devil card out of his coat, which he rolled between his fingers, faster and faster, his lips twitching with something dark and twisted.

"What do you mean?" For some unknown reason, a shiver went through my back, and my skin hissed on alert.

"I mean, flower goddess, if someone has the potential to destroy your kingdom, it is that you've never been the true ruler of it." He flicked his card, which flew away with the wind to fall in front of Carmin's store. "To be untouchable, you should never have a contestant."

"But if you're successful, people will want to make you fall." I shook my head, finally pulling away from the window. "They'll want to take everything you have."

"But they can't, can they?" His eyes glimmered, and the shadow on his face gave the impression his scar was expanding menacingly on his cheek. "That's the difference."

Radcliff's words stuck to my jaw while we ambled through the center of the place. Perhaps he was right. All you needed was to excel in your area without feeling threatened by anyone else. No one could take away who you are and your accomplishments. After all, creations and humans couldn't be compared, or else it'd inflict only self-doubt and misery.

"So, if my thing is scents…" I shot him a glance. "What is yours? Precious rocks and jewels, right? Or maybe your club?"

"I'll not reveal all my cards." Shadows seemed to dance above him as if the spirits of the night had awoken. "Not even to you, little witch."

I ignored the breaking feeling inside my heart and the fact his reply could only mean that Radcliff had darker purposes. Purposes he wasn't ready to share with me. Ones including the aphrodisiac.

We stopped at a fountain, the noise of the water leaping above my unwanted thoughts. I focused upon the imposing statue standing in the middle of the fountain. It was an angel, a fallen one, whose wings had been broken. Once upon a time, he had been white, but now he had black marks on him, like thorns tearing him apart. He had cracks everywhere, as if someone had tried to sew him back. His face was cut by a line in the middle, one of his eyes black. That angel had been through hell, but he was just as beautiful as the man next to me.

"He looks like you, somehow." I admired every inch of it. "Unique, scarred, and powerful."

"He's an angel." Radcliff squinted his eyes at the statue. "And not a good one as it seems."

"You know, I always thought we all had a guardian angel." Sadness washed over me in a wave, memories trying to rush back.

"Even if I lost mine. I'm not even mad he abandoned me. I deserved it."

Radcliff cracked his knuckles, his gaze not leaving the statue. "What happened?"

"He went away because of me." My voice trembled and weakened. I had never spoken to anyone about this before. "It was all my fault."

Radcliff crossed his arms on his chest, a visible frown on his forehead. He drifted his stare in my direction with icy coldness. "You met him?"

"No, I—" I sighed. "I don't remember. My memory is playing tricks on me. I'm not even sure he's a him—maybe none of that was real. The only thing I remember was the scent of him and the day he left. That plant."

"It's all in the past. It doesn't matter if it was an illusion or the truth." Radcliff's muscles stiffened.

"You're right." I peered up at the statue one last time. "It's funny, but now I think you could be some kind of guardian angel too." I smiled. "Some kind of hero."

"Just because I won't be the monster in your story doesn't mean I'll be your hero. I'm not. I'll never be. I'm the villain, Lily, and nothing will ever change that."

Chapter 15

Radcliff

A macabre image to wake up to:
A giant doll hung on the top floor of Carmin's headquarters.

This morning, the crowd rushed to the Carmin's empire. A giant doll or, more accurately, a spitting image of Carmin's CEO, Christian, was hung on the last floor of the building.

The doll with the effigy of Christian wore a white bathrobe emblazoned with his initials: CC. But that's not it. The word "rapist" was written in blood on his chest, disconcerting passers-by in the street.

The police took suspects working at Carmin's into custody. The culprit(s) would have entered the company and broken inside Christian Carmin's house to steal that bathrobe. Nothing else has been stolen to date inside his property.

Christian Carmin: A rapist.

The gloomy message yesterday calling out Carmin a rapist has caused a riot among families. Women have manifested in front of the building all morning with signs written: 'stop abuse,' 'we are not objects,' 'my body: my choice, not yours'.

Six women emerged from the silence, accusing Christian Carmin of rape, sexism and abuse. To quote a testimonial that froze our backs from a 17-year-old model, "he said he was going to help me and introduce me to his contacts. I believed him, and when he asked me to come to his office to talk, he forced me to give him a blowjob. He was getting off on my tears. I'm still ashamed. He was so powerful, and I was no one. Who would believe me?"

An investigation has been officially opened, causing the Carmins' company to fall considerably in the market, buyers no longer trusting the tainted image of the brand. Adonis Carmin, son of Carmin, spoke last night. "My dad would never be able to do such a thing. It's unthinkable. He's always been a loving dad and always respected women. That's why he created Carmin—to sublimate them, not rape them. He never used any type of violence. The employees love him. Someone is just trying to sabotage us since our recent expansion."

Now, the question we're all asking ourselves: Will this scandal condemn the luxury giant to go bankrupt?

A page of history is turning.

I crinkled tomorrow's newspaper into a ball—sent by another soul I owned working as an editor in chief—and tossed it into the fireplace.

Just like this news, Carmin would cease to exist and become nothing but dust and ashes.

All I needed to ignite the lightning was a spark.

People would take care of his destruction. All I had to do was to watch him fall. It was enough to point the light on Carmin, for his darkness and the truth to catch up with him. They would all come out of the silence, and although he managed to pay the most expensive lawyer and escape punishment with his little power, his company was dead. It was the first step in his destruction.

He knew it was me. The bathroom robe was a reminder.

When you have something to hide or lose, you can't afford to play with fire. He couldn't reach me.

This was my first check.

And soon, I'd say *checkmate*.

Chapter 16

Lily

Scent was the closest sense to the emotional brain. It made our memories speak the language of our soul. Scents were like falling in love, leading us to the complete dark to an unknown destination.

I would have been blind with the silky blindfold clouding my vision if it wasn't for my nose picking the floral and evergreen woodsy notes, sharing its vision with me. Radcliff and I were back on the flower fields. I could tell by the way my body relaxed under the lavender smells, washing away all my negative emotions. The way the explosive bouquet of white tuberose smelled of salt skin in summer and milky dreams.

"Open your eyes." His voice bloomed my senses, and I felt the weight of his haunting and transcending aura leaving my side.

I let go of the blindfold.

One minute ago, there was only darkness.

The wait.

The unknown.

Now, with opened eyes and no blindfold, it was only heaven.

"What is—" I stopped midsentence.

Radcliff had grabbed the handle of an old wooden door to what I believed to be an extraction plant because it was placed right in the middle of the flower fields. From the outside, it looked like an old countryside house, only bigger, the size of a small hangar. The windows were huge, letting the light enter. Its stone walls were covered with ivy, which climbed the facade.

Not far away from this, there was a Mediterranean *mas* or some kind of colored bastide with an orange facade and blue shutters, the ideal place to sit on a rocking chair and smell the fresh aroma of a morning sunrise, listening to the cicadas.

"I believe you already know," Radcliff answered my question and opened the door to a new universe.

He engulfed himself inside, and the sugary scent of roses filled my nostrils with the draft that called me in. I stepped inside the entrance of this magic kingdom, taking the whole place in. Huge copper tubs faced us. They were probably three meters tall, opened at the top, similar to an enormous cauldron to brew forbidden elixirs.

This was where magical potions were made.

The place where flowers became perfume.

A perfume factory.

The light pierced through the giant windows into radiant rays, giving the impression the tubs were enchanted with fairy dust floating around.

I was Alice in Wonderland.

"How do you have access to this place?" My voice echoed across the vastness of space.

Radcliff walked up the stone staircase that led to the first floor. The mezzanine overlooked the copper tubs.

A cynical smile tipped his lips. "This property belongs to your fields."

My eyes opened wildly, and a scream of excitement escaped my mouth. "So, this is all mine?"

"You need a place to make your perfume oils, if I'm not mistaken?" Radcliff arrived at the mezzanine and leaned on the railing of the metallic balcony.

I couldn't believe this. The fields of flowers in Grasse were linked to the biggest names in the perfume world. It was the only place for a perfumer to be. The climate that hit the land brought magic to the blooms; it was unique in the world. The fields were often bought by an extraction plant, so the flower pickers would harvest the blooms at the first ray of sun to bring them inside the copper tub for their petals to become precious oils. Usually, a nearby villa would—

"This and the bastide next to it belong to you. It's small but enough for one person," he added.

"What?" It wasn't small—it was huge. "It's perfect! Oh my god! I'm living a dream. Is it real? No way, it can't be real! This is insane!" A flood of unstoppable speech escaped my lips.

He offered me on a hellish platter more than I could dare to dream about and hope for. But I needed to remind myself that with Radcliff, nothing came without a price. The Devil makes deals, not fairy-tale dreams come true.

"But I shouldn't accept that…" I murmured, putting my elation to a halt.

"Perhaps you shouldn't." With assurance, he gave a sign of his hand for me to come up. "But we both know you'll never refuse my *gift*."

He was right—there was no need to lie. I would accept it without looking back twice. I'd sacrifice everything to build a kingdom of my own. Hell, I'd already sold my soul for a scent.

But still, a part of me wondered why Radcliff would do that for me. Why would he care about my happiness so much if he was truly unable to love someone? No actions were selfless, but I refused to believe this one was only about possession.

"You said if I were to leave, you'd burn the world except for a land of flowers you'd show mercy on. Because you knew that's where I'd be. Is it your assurance to find your way back to me?"

"We both know I have some controlling and protective tendencies." Hence, his personal bodyguards guarding the field. "But like I said, this is a gift."

He understood my dream and the fire that animated my soul.

"I thought the Devil didn't give gifts?" I teased him, taking the stairs.

"Not when it's about his queen."

Queen. That name made my heart stop like a bomb exploding, freezing me into place. I seized the railing, my eyes locking with his. He didn't shift; if anything, he grew more imposing by his statement, his smell tinting the room of night-blooming flowers and ghoulish skeletal specters. I swallowed, a wave of goose bumps traveling through my face to my legs.

I had probably become scarlet red, imagining myself reigning on a throne of thorny carnivorous blossoms in the midst of hell. I continued climbing up the stairs, and once upstairs, his hand reaching out to me was an invitation I couldn't refuse.

The moment our hands sealed together, it felt like he was introducing me to his invisible royal subjects, a court of phantoms and the undead.

He gave me a nod, and I leaned forward on the ramp, gazing inside the giant cauldron. The ballerina-pink centifolia roses filled only a few centimeters of the tub. The other two were filled out to the top. I inhaled the scents, a feeling of enchantment and wonder transpiercing me—this was the epitome of spring.

"I want to go inside." I leaned the most that I could over the ramp, my hair falling to the top of the cauldron. "Do you think I could jump?"

"Not without hurting yourself."

"Oh," I breathed, not hiding my disappointment.

"But…" He trailed off. I instantly looked backward at him. Radcliff loomed behind me and caged me in with his arms before his lips curved into a sly sneer. "There is perhaps another way if you look closely."

He glanced at the cauldron one last time, then to me. I refocused on the tub, squinting, my eyes zooming between every detail until my stare captured a little door at the bottom, halfway hidden by the roses. I gasped, and Radcliff's arms freed me, allowing me to bolt down the stairs.

I got around the impressive tub, searching for that small door—it wasn't much taller than a meter at the most. I was truly Alice in Wonderland, but luckily for me, I wouldn't need a potion to be able to get inside of it.

I stopped in front of the copper door, tilting my neck back to peer at Radcliff upstairs. "Is it locked?"

He leaned his elbows over the railing, his eyes glittering with twisted amusement. I grabbed the handle and turned it slowly. Once the secret passage opened, a few roses fell to the ground. I slipped inside on my knees and enclosed the door behind me to keep the flowers inside. One thing was for sure, Radcliff would never be able to come through it.

I was in the middle of the roses like I was inside my own castle, and my chin quivered under the emotions of happiness that took root in me. I held a few flowers in my palms, sniffing them. I was so ecstatic that I laughed and threw them in the air. I watched the roses fly as if they were shooting stars. Once they fell back, they mingled with my hair, blessing me with their aroma.

I craned my neck back to Radcliff with the most dazzling of smiles. "This is heaven!"

I fell into the bath of flowers, which held me like arms so I could lie in this bed of dreamy pink. Radcliff grabbed a few petals from another tub and slid them between his fingers with an amused grin. This was probably the only natural smile he'd ever given me. It wasn't controlled, nor artificial. It was honest and free.

One by one, the petals met my skin, and I rose up, catching them like a child on a quest. I succeeded in taking one and pinned it behind my ear as a trophy. My laugh echoed in the shed, and I whirled around until I felt dizzy, wanting to be consumed by this sweet madness.

"I don't want to leave this place," I chuckled, taking another turn faster. "You should come!"

I spun and spun until the shades of pink and copper blurred my vision. I looked back at Radcliff when I noticed his shadow wasn't on the balcony anymore. "Radcliff?"

I stopped spinning, coming back to my senses slowly.

Why didn't he say something?

There was only silence.

"Radcliff, where are—"

Hands snatched my waist.

A whisper tingled my neck.

Warmth invaded my core.

"Right behind you." His lips teased my ear in a haunting breath.

In a second, he had reeled me around, and I crashed on his hard chest with a hammering heart that would defy all the laws of the cosmos. Like two opposites attracting, Radcliff's pitch-black aura met my pink, floral one and the probably crimson of my cheek. I craned my neck to the balcony. *How did he jump?* I hadn't heard him, nor seen him. I plunged into the darkest pit of his eyes, short on breath, trying to solve the mystery that he truly was.

He is the Devil that captured my soul.

The monster that blossomed my heart.

The man that bloomed every dying root in me.

Lost in the purple calla lily of his eyes like he belonged to another galaxy far away from my universe, I craved to reveal the enchantment he had bounded me with. "How did you do this? How did you come to—"

He cut me off with a kiss, the kind that made the earth shatter and rip apart. A kiss that would explode our hearts into tiny particles floating around us so he could steal them afterward. He would stitch them together to form a new heart that he would plant in my chest and empty his.

He eclipsed all the questions in my mind and made our demons dance in heaven as he pinned me against the wall of the cauldron, my legs wrapped instinctively around his waist. I was possessed by something stronger than desire. An emotion that had consumed me whole, one that had taken root in me for some time and grown to be as destructive as it was beautiful.

He cupped my jaw with dominance, and his lips branded my mouth again and again, binding me with him. Our tongues swiveled into a hot tango, one that would lift every corpse around us by the intensity of our flicks. That kiss belonged to dark magic.

We fed on our demons, craving to bleed the other as a contract inked in blood. I yearned to hurt him as much as he yearned to hurt me—with possession, passion, and care. But that kiss was also our humanities taming each other, learning to trust and exchange hearts. Light and dark in an eternal battle.

My fingers intertwined in his sleek hair, pushing him toward me with a longing for more. As for him, he had seized my waist to the point of breaking me, mastering perfectly the fine line between pain and pleasure.

He cupped my breasts over the top of my summer dress before releasing them. His lips left mine to close on my nipple, worshipping me by sucking, nibbling, licking.

I moaned under the danger of freeing Radcliff's humanity. I wanted it all. The bad. The ugly. The twisted. The hopeful. The mix of his earthy scent with the roses was like the most enchanting contrast inebriating my senses.

I unzipped the fly of his pants, and he uncuffed my wrist, which banged against the copper wall.

"I hope you weren't attached to this dress," he threatened with the rasp of his voice.

A tearing sound echoed. Radcliff had ripped the middle bottom of my dress in one strong grip, exposing my panties. A bolt of electricity rushed through my veins, and I raked my nails over his satin shirt.

"I hope you weren't attached to your fancy shirt," I countered, cocking an eyebrow. I opened it in the same animalistic way as he did with my floral dress, breaking each of his buttons.

I licked my lips, observing all of his godly body. I caressed his strong abs, coming across his scars that aroused me. They were maps of his past. His strength. Him.

"Let's see if you're wet, little witch." He sucked on my lower lip and took off my panties by ripping them on the side, losing them in the flowers.

His finger teased my folds, and I gasped, holding my breath. My shameless wetness pooled over him. A satisfied grin took hold of his lips, and he slapped my sex, making me jump against the wall. He licked the taste of me, the chaos in his eyes satiated.

"Very wet," the Devil teased. "Just the way I want you to be. That, and red as the reminiscence of the way I own you in a way no one will ever." He slapped my butt cheek, and desire pounded in my clit. "Red and messy with pleasure, in a way you'll never be able to forget how I've possessed you every time you look at yourself in a mirror." He pinched my nipple before sliding his finger over the valley between my breasts. "I also want your madness. Your darkness. Your obsession. Everything. Even the air you breathe."

Our eyes sank into each other, into the darkest abyss of ourselves. For a short moment, I could read him as clear as a crystal ball, his being opening up to me like puzzle pieces coming together. I saw his pain. His needs. His cravings. His darkness, as magnificent as stars shining in the most chaotic of skies.

And I saw me.

His weakness, possessing his heart.

Taking me by the waist, he lifted me with his nonhuman strength so that my thighs rested on his shoulders and his head at the height of my sex.

"What are you doing?" I blushed, looking downward at him.

"Worshiping you, of course." He lowered his mouth to my aching sex before kissing my crotch, his hand taking hold of my leg. "From hell to heaven."

When his mouth closed on my clit, my fingers immediately clutched on his hair, and my gasp echoed in the hangar. The butterflies in my belly flew widely to the point they combusted in fireworks at the feel of the work of art that was his tongue.

I rolled my hips with a pulsing clit and clenching muscles. He devoured me like a spell that couldn't be undone, creating an inferno inside me. He didn't look away from me as my chest leaped with each of his touches.

I was drawn to the void, leaning toward it, wanting to give in to my pleasure. My eyelids fluttered, and I met his pace, spasms contracting my stomach. I lost control and let myself collapse to hit the merciless ground.

But Radcliff's strong grip on my waist prevented me from falling, holding me firmly against the copper wall. Protective and destructive, he increased his pace, my heartbeat pounding.

Each flick of his tongue sent a firebolt over my clit, and a red jolt of lust consumed me entirely. "Rad—I... Don't stop."

His final note sent me to heaven as he promised, and stars clouded my vision. My orgasm arrived at full speed, in a way it couldn't be tamed or contained. Radcliff nonetheless maintained his pace, letting my orgasm crash again and again at an intensity I couldn't hold. My legs shook, my belly contracting, and I held on to the copper wall, short of breath.

When he pulled away, I found my breath again, and I relaxed my muscles into his hold. I was a red mess, and he was my madness.

"You're my Devil," I whispered. My guardian angel had traded places with the Devil. The one that was meant to match my darkness. "Perhaps we were destined to meet."

Holding me, he made me fall into his arms, keeping me locked in his embrace. Our eyes met, our heartbeats beating in sync. I wrapped my legs around his torso, a hoard of goose bumps informing me that it was now too late to back away from the link uniting us.

"You were born for me, Lily." He caressed away the sweaty strands of my hair that had fallen over my forehead, observing me with an intensity that made my legs go weak. "Just like I was meant for you. Now, say that you're mine, little witch."

"Make me," I ordered. "Show me how black your heart is and how it beats only for me."

I want your humanity. Your soul.

He laughed darkly and grazed his finger around my breast, a single touch that had the power to direct all my cells. "With pleasure."

"Give me your worst, Radcliff," I provoked him with a smile.

In the space of one breath, he slammed into me, my head hitting the cauldron at the feel of him, as if a hurricane had carried me to another world. Together, we crossed the most powerful tide to overdo the elements of nature and broke the boundaries of space and time.

My back slammed against the wall, and I bit my lower lip almost as hard as his hand squeezed my butt cheek. His other hand held me in place so he could hit the deepest part of me. Our lips sealed in a kiss that spoke thousands of dark love poems.

Fuck. Fuck. Fuck. My mind spiraled out of control. With each of his thrusts, he stole my soul and took my heart with it. I was helpless for him, governed by my carnal need, raking my nails over his back, digging them in until he bled. He was my aphrodisiac, my own dose of destruction and madness.

His hand seized my throat, and I surrendered willingly to his possession. He nibbled on my lower lip before breaking our kiss for our breaths to increase into groans and moans. We breathed the same air, stealing each other's, and I rocked my hips to meet his hard, merciless drives.

His strong arm wrapped against my waist still held me in place as he devoted his attention to my neck, savoring me. I felt my body vaping into thin air, as if I were a flower whose petals flew in the wind. I gave him twice the chaos that he demanded, obeying his silent orders. My hips moved to his will, and my eyes yearned to shut under the intensity. My body clenched—he was driving me to the point of madness, when pleasure couldn't be held or tamed. I'd explode. It was too consuming. Too good. Too—

"Radcliff," I screamed when he hit the end of me, and I felt him deep in my belly.

He palmed my breast, and my eyebrows knit together, pleasure increasing in waves. When I thought it'd be the final strikes, he decreased his pace, slow but deep. It almost hurt. That longing. That need to come.

I tempted him by bringing my chest closer by squeezing my arms. I wanted to take his control, to make him long for me as much as he teased me. I moaned, licking my lips, knowing that I'd draw his attention to them.

"Oh, little witch." Radcliff gave a slap to my breast, and my belly clenched in reply. "What are you trying to achieve?"

Winning. I wanted to bring him to the edge. To the edge between emotions and desire. To the edge that would revive his soul. Control was a way to protect yourself; I wanted him to give it up, for me, but he could see right through my game.

"Punishment is what you want?" When he did it again, my breasts instinctively inched forward to him, wanting more of him. "No, there is something else." He punished me by pulling my nipple toward him with his forefingers.

In his eyes, I saw his battle underneath. The monster in him had a scar that had reddened, veins on his forehead and eyes so dark that no one could defy him. The other side, his human one, seemed almost afraid. Afraid to feel more than he ever had. Afraid to lose his power.

That side of him was slowly disappearing, consumed by the monster. Determined to not let him hide behind his mask once more at the price of losing both of him, I had to speak the only words he could understand.

"I'm yours," I admitted on a moan. "I'm unconditionally yours."

A tear threatened to appear on the corner of my eyes, but I blinked it away. Radcliff's eyes roamed my face, searching for the truth. A truth he didn't seem to believe.

"I'm yours," I articulated again with the softness of my voice.

This time, he thrust harder into me with abandon, making me jump against the copper wall. When my pleasure built up, I knew

I'd explode. My body shivered. I was bound to Radcliff just like he was bound to me. No matter the outcome or the choices we would make, there was no escape in this life.

We created eternity, enslaving ourselves to each other.

At that moment, flower petals dropped from the ceiling. They fell down on us like a magical rain. I looked up to see a small basket was upended, and a little string was holding it. This was where the flowers were coming from. But how? I hadn't seen anything inside the tub that could have actioned it.

"How?" I murmured, my eyes boring on Radcliff.

"Magic?" He drew a sinister line, the petals passing by his face.

"You're an enigma," I responded, my eyebrows slithering inward under the burning heat filling my insides. Radcliff couldn't be human. He was something else. Something powerful and mystical, unbound by the rules of this world.

"And you'll be my downfall. My weakness."

My throat dried, and his pace increased, sending me back to his hellish kingdom. My nails dug into his hair. The flowers continued on falling, and my orgasm took me apart in a last scream that made me look to heaven. Radcliff broke against my wave, his orgasm overpowering mine. Time seemed to stop as I melted into him, hearing only the sound of my hammering heart, my ears buzzing.

The Devil had made love to the flower goddess.

The monster had owned the heart of the witch.

I obtained my dream and much more than I could ever have imagined with him, but that happiness wouldn't last until tomorrow. All magic comes at a price, and Radcliff was my magic.

I knew that going back home, a choice should be made.

A choice that could change everything.

A choice between dreams and hearts.

Chapter 17

Lily

The cold, oceanic air of Ravencliff Manor had filled my insides with dark myths and ghost stories.

I was back to the place where white became gray, and black ruled over the light. A place that was hidden in the fog if it wasn't for the ravens stiffening like gargoyles on the peaks from the roof of the manor that were as sharp as the blades of swords.

And in the midst of this gothic nightmare, a garnet aphrodisiac was born. A feral weapon that would taint the world in destructive desire. My heart slammed in my chest as I put the forbidden vial back in the cold.

It was ready.

My hands got sweaty at the thought of having to break the

news to Radcliff. To give me the courage, I grabbed the other vial containing my heaven-sent perfume. I let its smell transport me one last time as I opened the tube. A smile crossed my lips, and tingling strokes caressed me. It smelled of romantic waltzes inside a secret garden and torrid passion on satin sheets. Of falling from the sky to land inside a dark angel's arms. Of a blown dandelion reaching a land of folklore creatures and fairy tales, taking away with it your dearest wish. And most importantly, of *him*.

His story. From his darkness to his hellions, passing by his kingdom and wicked soul to land on the origin of his pain and beauty. I blinked, breaking out of the tale the scents were spellbinding me with. I wrapped my perfume in a burgundy cloth before securing it in a box. I still had a long way to go: find the packaging and market it to the world.

Despite everything that happened, I wanted to share the exciting news of my masterpiece with the people close to me—Adonis and my uncle. I rushed in the direction of the greenhouse, remembering I had dropped my phone there before my trip to Grasse.

The melodious, sad lullaby of the wind blew my hair away from my face and made me struggle to reach my sanctuary. With every step I took, a squall pulled me back, forbidding me to trespass its sacred ground. The greenhouse seemed to be guarded by an evil spell.

After clearing my way in spite of the stormy wind, my hand froze on the doorknob. My nostrils flared. A wave of death crept through me. *No.* Something was different. The smell, it was rotten like the flesh of a corpse and ashes.

I wrenched open the door, and a scream tore me apart. "No!"

The piercing shrieks of the ravens echoed through the greenhouse in a scream that hurt my ears. They cloaked my flower in shades of black, like an army of undead attacking her. The windows were broken from the top, the scenery morbid and terrifying. It was the most macabre of fate.

"Go away!" I rushed toward the Devil's Corpse, trying to make my way through the famished ravens.

There were at least twenty of them, devouring my flower with their stiff beaks. They fed on her carcass without pity, tearing her pretty leaves and blooms. They were soulless monsters, committing the most atrocious of crimes.

"Stop!" They didn't listen to me but hovered around me to prevent me from stepping forward. "Please, stop!"

I finally fell on my knees, covering my eyes with my hands for fear of being scratched. The ravens were driven mad. I fought to take a last glance at the Devil's Corpse, or the rest of it, despite the ravens circling me in their dark nightmares. I wondered why she didn't defend herself with her traps and thorns.

"Why are you doing this?" I yelped, my voice breaking. "Fight. Please."

It was almost as if she was inflicting this on herself.

She didn't respond to me.

A shot of anger pierced through me, and I rushed like a madwoman through the unkindness of ravens. "Go away! Leave her alone!"

They clawed at me, but I leaped in front of the plant, protecting her like a shield. My eyes shut and bled with tears of blood on my cheeks. Their gurgling croaks made me deaf. The world became dark and colorless, smelling like shooting stars collapsing on the earth to become dust.

I curse you.

I curse you to go back to hell where you came from.

In the middle of this nothingness, I no longer felt the ravens' wings flapping behind my back. Their howling dissipated to leave room for silence, and opening my eyes, I saw the ravens had retreated to the blue sky.

After that, calm reigned like the song of the dead after

bloodshed. It was carnage. I turned to face the fallen plant. She wouldn't survive.

"Why?" I touched her torn leaves, glared at her crushed blooms and at her roots emerging from the ground. "Why did you have to die… You could have defended yourself. Why didn't you…"

I sniffed, blinking the tears away in a silent goodbye to the flower that had changed my life.

I faced this gloomy scene in silence, mourning the dead.

I stomped toward Radcliff's office with dried tears on my cheeks. My eyes were bloodshot, my steps on the floor echoing in heavy clomps. The walls seemed to narrow as I approached, locking me in their pain. I hadn't even had the strength to open the messages I had received on my phone yet. I wasn't in the mood for happy birthday wishes and good news anymore. I wanted answers.

I slammed open the door of his office to find him enthroned to his desk. His gaze widened at the ghostly sight of me, and he shut off his computer and moved away whatever paper he was working on. He rose from his seat with a visible frown. "What happened?"

"The Devil's Corpse." I swallowed, inhaling deep. "She died. She was ripped apart. Eaten by ravens. They broke the windows of the greenhouse in their madness, and—" I stopped, my eyes stuck on nowhere, enslaved by the macabre memory. "They devoured her."

"So, it happened," he replied, as if that was something that was meant to be.

"Sorry?" My voice was tight, my eyes shooting flames of rage at the icy man in front of me. "What do you mean by 'it happened'?"

"There was a legend about the Devil's Corpse." He reeled around to look at the murder scene from his window. "She chooses when she's ready to die. And in doing so, she offers her flesh to animals who devour every last bit of her. It's an offered sacrifice. She decided her time was up."

"But that's barbaric! Inhumane!" I spluttered.

"No one makes the rules of nature. That's life and the price of death."

I shook my head, joining him by the window. "This is stupid."

"Or brave in a way. Perhaps it was a message." Radcliff went back to his desk, resuming his activities.

I gulped my feelings, thinking this through. "A message…"

The aphrodisiac and the perfume were ready. Could it be it? On her day of death, could she have wanted to see the light? Could I honor her death by making this day a glorious one? I unlocked my phone, set on announcing the news. I'd make her immortal and unforgettable.

I didn't open the messages from my uncle, from which the preview was "Did you see what happened to the Carmins?" because I was bored of his obsession with them. I opened the unread messages from Adonis instead.

Yesterday, 10pm.

Adonis: Happy birthday, Lily. I'm thinking about you. I hope you're having a special day. Wanna hang out tomorrow?

Today, 8am.

Adonis: Are you okay?

My eyes swiveled to the upcoming message, my heart leaping into my throat, about to combust.

No.

The earth seemed to have ripped open, dragging me into the endless dark. My hand frantically grabbed the curtain next to me as I felt myself spinning.

"Lily?" Radcliff called out to me, but his voice was distant and blurry.

The last message from Adonis was fatal.

Today, 5pm.

Adonis: So, you get on your knees in front of the Devil but you don't even bother to reply to me? For info…

I opened the attached picture. It was an invitation that Radcliff had sent to Adonis.

Mr. Adonis Carmin, you're invited by Mr. Radcliff for a meeting at 9pm today at Club 7. It's a onetime invitation.

Betrayal was all I felt reading the next message, acid burning my throat.

Three words.

Three words that meant everything.

Adonis: I saw you.

"Lily?" Radcliff's voice buzzed through my ears.

Adonis might have seen me giving a blowjob to Radcliff that night at the club, but more importantly, Radcliff knew that all along. He did it on purpose. My hand fisted the curtain, and I refused to let the salty tears of anger bleed on my skin. Radcliff had used me to get his revenge on Adonis.

I wasn't his equal.

I was his puppet.

I finally met Radcliff's eyes, an expression of disgust twisting my features. I wanted to blow up this fucking place. I was an idiot.

"How could you!" I screamed.

He didn't even flinch, keeping his regal calm. "You'll have to be more precise."

"Adonis!" I yelled hysterically. "You invited him to your club that night! You knew he was there when we…" The next words stuck in my throat.

"I did." He didn't bother to hide the truth and adjusted his cuffs. "It was a matter between him and I that needed to be solved."

"You used me." My single tear finally escaped as I pushed him away, hatred consuming my core.

"He defied me when he came to my property. I told you he'd pay. I'm the Devil, Lily—this is what I do. I cannot be weak." He clenched his teeth. "He needed to let go of you. To understand."

"Understand what?" I pushed him again violently, and a muscle in his jaw knotted, trying to keep his anger in check. Either way, I couldn't care less about it. "That I'm your puppet? A toy?"

"You're mine," he roared.

"You don't own me," I spat out.

"But I do, Lily." A snarl drew on his lips like a lethal weapon. "We're bound together whether we want it or not."

"You're delusional and crazy if you think that."

"Who's the crazier of us, Lily? The one that resurrected the humanity of a monster or the one who was one all along?"

"You're not even regretting this?" My mouth twitched.

"I could have killed him, but I didn't."

I snorted, not believing his words. "And I should thank you for that? You're unbelievable!"

His jaw tightened, and the ridges of his neck became dangerously pronounced. "I've never pretended to be someone I'm not with you."

A man without a soul with a heart blackened by hatred.

This time, I believed him. He was the villain all along. "You've hurt me—did you think of that at least one second? Did you get off at the thought of—"

"I can't be weak, not even for you. It was his punishment, the worst that could happen to him," he shouted. "Don't you understand? I'd fucking die for you, bleed, and kill, Lily. You're fucking consuming me. All those emotions, I don't know what to do with them. You scarred me even more than I already was." He brought his fist to his mouth, his hellions gathering. "I give you my heart, but my soul, Lily, I don't have one to offer you."

So, that was it. The brutal truth. Radcliff didn't know how to love. He could not love. He was never taught how, and now, that newborn humanity was killing him. Those feelings were new for him, and he let them overwhelm him. I had unleashed the worst of his humanity.

"You were jealous of Adonis. The *great* Radcliff was jealous of someone, who knew," I joked sarcastically with a snort.

"I was not." The way he clenched his teeth and the vein popping on his forehead meant it wasn't entirely true. "Did you know that your coward Junior has been trying to approach me for weeks for a meeting? He's been annoyingly stubborn. So, I naturally gave him what he wanted."

"What?" That news made me choke on my own breath.

"Like a little kid, he holds me responsible for his daddy's downfall and for the way I *corrupted* you." The word "corrupted" rolled off his tongue, sweet and wicked.

I thought of what had happened to the Carmins lately. The fact that Adonis's father was beaten. The problems with Carmin's enterprise. The secret I had confessed to Radcliff.

A cold shiver crept beneath my spine, and I unlocked my phone again with trembling hands. When I opened the message from my uncle, all doubts became clear, and all scents became dusty grays. There were articles: *A giant doll hung on the top floor of Carmin's headquarters; Christian Carmin: the rapist.*

A doll with the bathrobe Christian had worn the day he tried to touch me. The one with his initials embroidered.

Only one man was capable of this kind of wrath and chaos.

"Did you?" My voice shivered. "Did you have something to do with the Carmins?"

Radcliff inched forward, towering over me with his darkness. "Deeper. You already know the answer."

Yes. He was responsible.

"They never did anything wrong to you…" I slanted my

eyebrows inward, feeling stupid to have believed in the light within Radcliff. "Why would you destroy someone's life for your pleasure?"

"I did it for you, Lily." His mouth shut tight and grim, his eyes burning like hellfire.

"For me? Yeah, right." I tried to get away from him, his arms, his scent, his everything, but he held me caged between his arms. "The Carmins didn't deserve this! You're just—"

"You think everyone is so pure? Look around you—everyone lied to you. You're too blind to see the truth."

"And you don't have any faith in humans," I quipped back. "Because you can only see how repulsive and inhuman you are!"

Fuck. A wave of regret engulfed me, knowing there was no turning back from the venom I spread.

"Repulsive? Is that what I am to you?" His eyes turned cruel, as sharp as blades, and the corners of his lips lifted up into something dark and scary. "Did you know that your fucking uncle sold your mother's perfume right after her death to Carmin?"

My mouth dropped. "What?"

For a moment, Radcliff's expression twisted with surprise. He'd never meant to let this slide.

"Which perfume, Radcliff?" I articulated, fury springing to life inside me.

"The 27."

My favorite perfume.

The perfume whose nose identity was the most well-guarded secret of Carmin. No one ever knew who it was.

I felt like I'd been stabbed by a knife into my heart and some corrosive liquid was tearing me up from the inside—slowly and painfully, like the most maleficent of thorns.

"I don't believe you." *I can't believe you.* "She didn't—it's not possible. You're lying!"

"Now, why would I lie to you?" His nostrils flared, a muscle in his jaw working. "I have proof. A conversation recorded with your uncle."

So, it is true.

Radcliff would never speak of proof if he didn't have any.

In some way, it all made sense, as if my heart always knew— that's why it hurt so much. Who apart from my mother could have created a perfume so enchanting and magical? Only she had the talent for it.

But she would have never wanted her creation to be stolen and become someone else's. I knew that because I was just like her. My uncle had betrayed me and my mother, stealing her legacy and achievement for his own gain, but why? For money and fame? *How could he be so greedy.*

Radcliff wasn't any better. He had lied to me all this time. He knew too. Everything had been a lie. Radcliff was right—I was too blind. Christian had taken my mother's masterpiece from me without shame, claiming it as his own. My head spun, and my nose seemed invaded by spicy scents that burnt me.

"Why did you never tell me this?" I swallowed my anger and the pound of hatred tapping in my chest.

"It wasn't my secret to tell. It would only hurt you. The past is best buried and—"

"The reason I came to Ravencliff Manor," I cut him off, closing my eyes for a second to not give him the pleasure to witness my tears. I opened them again, determined to get the whole truth out this time. "Is that why you chose me to make the aphrodisiac? Because you knew about my mother."

Radcliff nodded.

He had chosen me because of my mother's talent, not the faith he had in me.

"Before meeting you on New Year's Eve, yes," he said as emotionless as he was.

Sweet Lily was consumed by a volcano about to erupt and starved to inflict chaos. Radcliff had awoken my darkest side, and now, they'd all pay for it—that was a promise. I eclipsed all my emotions, locking them inside my Pandora's box. I would unleash them when I was ready to get justice.

"I entered into a war with Carmin for what he did to you." Radcliff clenched his fist, his face hard. "I'm on your side, Lily."

"It's not your war." My eyes reddened, and anger shouted a rush of adrenaline through my veins. "I need to go."

He held my wrist, keeping me from leaving. "Don't."

"You can't give me one reason to stay." I was done with my disillusion.

He thought this through before articulating one word that seemed to rip him apart. "Me."

"Oh yeah?" I paused with a raised eyebrow, the corners of my lips turning up. "Will you choose me over the aphrodisiac, Radcliff?"

"You know how it feels to want revenge so badly on... everything." He towered closer, trying to manipulate me with his intoxicating aroma. But I wouldn't take his side anymore. I would take mine and mine alone. "I need to show them how weak they are. They need to pay. I need to expose their true colors. I can't renounce it."

He was a masochist, taking pleasure in inflicting pain on the sinners—the same kind of people that inflicted pain on him during his childhood. He was playing god, bringing his own sense of justice.

"This is again about your father? He's still owning you, Radcliff. If you release the aphrodisiac, it'll destroy you too. I've smelled it—it's pure chaos. A concentrate of darkness. Only one drop and it'll reveal and amplify the worst inside you. You'll create monsters. It's like dropping a nuclear bomb on humanity."

"Perhaps this is exactly what I want," he retorted, being the soulless man he promised he'd be. "It'd change everything."

"Then, I don't want to witness any of this. What's the goal to have all this power if it's for being a lonely god?" Because I would never stand by his side as the goddess of hell and destruction. Not anymore. I wouldn't witness his downfall, the step too far that would take away from his redemption.

"If you had to choose between your perfume and me, Lily, what would you choose? If you had to give up something." He squinted his eyes, already knowing the answer.

The window of his office slammed open. The cold air burst inside and swayed my hair, but our burning stares remained locked on each other. The elements were meddling in our war, the sky grounding our hatred.

"You can't compare the aphrodisiac with the perfume, Radcliff. One is pure evil while the other—"

"Both are for selfish uses. There is no light without darkness, Lily, just like there is no right and wrong. Do you think it's *right* that these people don't get punished for their crimes? You think it's *right* that they get to hide who they are and therefore deprive others of the ugly truth?"

He was gnawed by hatred. The blackness had ensnared his soul so deeply that no one could reach him anymore.

I finally answered his question with a knot in my throat. "I can't give up my dream."

I wouldn't give up everything I'd accomplished. It would always be my dream. It was the reason I was still alive.

A sinister grin curved his lips. "See, we're the same. Ambitious and wicked. With me, I'd never ask you to give up your obsession. I'd encourage you to chase after it. You'll be free to show who you truly are. Dark and—"

"I'm not dark." I refused to believe it.

"I know your thoughts and how you feel. I know your pain. Your betrayal. I read your soul. I can help you get revenge. Together, we'll—"

"This is not me!" I screamed. "I'm not you, Radcliff. I refuse to become like you."

I refused to give up on hope and humanity. I would seek revenge for my mother, but I would never take his path, or else I'd risk losing my soul too.

"Why did you make the aphrodisiac, then? You could have left. The day you jumped from the cliff, I gave you a choice. Why didn't you?" He squinted his eyes, his mouth thinning.

"Because I couldn't give up my dream, and I... I wanted to save you," I admitted with a trembling voice. "I didn't know the effects the aphrodisiac would have on humans back then, but I thought by giving you what you wanted, I could save your soul. That I could show you that life was much more than that."

Radcliff let out a thin laugh. "You wanted the weak human behind the beast. You're delusional."

"No, I wanted every part of you. The monster, the human, and the Devil. I never wanted to change you, but you've let your hatred and the memory of your father kill your entire being. You're stuck in the past. You're worth better than this. But you're right," I added. "I can't ask you to renounce who you are, just like I can't give up everything for you. I could beg you to not release the aphrodisiac, but it wouldn't change your mind. I get it. I get you. I get why you feel that you have to do this. But our universes are too opposite, Radcliff."

Together, we were a destructive outcome from the start.

The worst part of it all was that his darkness attracted me as much as the tiny bit of light that resided in him.

"We're taking opposite roads," I whispered. "This... it's not possible."

Radcliff didn't try to change my mind. Instead, he went back to the window, watching the nightmares he was bound to. He knew I was right and that we were both wrong for indulging us to exist in the first place. We were an illusion, and now we'd have to get back to the scentless reality.

"I always knew you'd be my downfall, Lily."

And I always knew I would lose my heart to him, and that one day, he'd break it.

"I need to leave, Radcliff." I didn't let the chaos inside me show through.

He turned his head, his profile only visible to me. "Don't you understand? You'll never be able to leave."

"So, you'll hold me prisoner in a golden cage?" My voice was laced with bitterness.

"No, I'll let you go if it's what you wish, but your soul will always be bound with me. I'll be in your head and dreams. Us, it will never end. I warned you there was no escape. For any of us."

"I know."

And that's how I turned to never look back at Ravencliff Manor and left my heart with the monster.

For eternity.

Chapter 18

Radcliff

Lily was gone from my world.

She had rejoined the place she belonged to, her land of flowers under the daylight while I remained hidden in the moonlight underworld.

A blur appeared at the window of my club, like a hellish fog sealing the fate of this place.

I squinted at the depraved crowd and their pitiful existence. I wanted them all fucking gone. It was almost morning, and here they were, consuming the illusion I designed for them. Human nature wasn't worth saving—except for her.

A knot in my throat tightened, preventing my monstrous breathing from filling the air with death and tenebrosity. I had let

Lily go because it was the right thing to do. How ironic that it was the only right thing I'd done in my wretched life, and I was paying the price for it by being miserable.

That wouldn't be the end. Lily knew I'd always find her. She'd never be free of me, as much as she haunted me.

We were a curse.

But for now, I had revenge to execute. A small liquid that could change the fate of humanity. A liquid bound with witchcraft. A cruel scowl twisted my features. They'd soon bow to their desires and impulses, showing the weakness of human nature in all its ugliness. They'd be dependent, exposing their sins and the worst of them in plain sight. Father would be proud.

The countdown had started.

The vial was secured in my box that I hid inside a special locker on the wall. There was no coming back from it. I'd defy the gods and bring to Earth the monsters in hell. My soon-to-be hellions would cause chaos, and all of them would lose everything.

"I'm done." Guessing by the sound of heels resonating on the floor of my office, I deduced it was Melissa. As for the loud noise that made me fist my hand, it was probably a broom that had landed on the doorstep.

I turned around, amusement flickering at the view of Melissa wearing that orange prison-cell jumpsuit that was out of fashion. Yet, she had managed to wear high stripper heels with a huge belt and other leather accessories, trying to rearrange the ugliness of that outfit. It didn't work. Not even with the way she curved her hips sideways, thrusting her hands on them, nor her plunging neckline.

"Do it again, then." I wasn't in the mood to entertain anyone.

"I'm tired!" She took off her shoes, wincing, before swinging her heels to the floor in an unseductive gesture. A sigh of relief appeared on her lips, and she let go of her femme fatale posture, hunching her shoulders. "These goddamn hurt!" She then leaned against the door. "You won, okay? Can I get my old job back, please? I'll beg and do whatever it takes."

"I never change a contract." I crossed my arms, unmoved by that capricious display. "But if you continue to bother me, you'll have a worse fate."

She shook her head and chewed her inner lip. "She's gone, isn't she?"

"Who," I growled between clenched teeth, about to murder Hugo for gossiping.

"Your happily ever after," she snorted. "I didn't see her tonight, and you have that look."

"What. Look."

"Miserable kind." She raised her brow, thinking she was entertaining me. "A mix of go fuck yourself and I'm gonna drown myself in a lake wearing my wedding tux."

"Get. Back. To. Work." My veins boiled with irritation. Every bad part of me hissed, on the verge of letting out my evilness.

"I used to have the same look thinking of you, before," she dropped in a whisper that seemed almost sincere and vulnerable.

"Melissa—"

"For what it's worth…" she dared to cut me off, sauntering past my office slowly, her nails raking the windows into a grinding sound. "I warned you. She couldn't accept all of you—she wasn't meant to be with you. She's good, and you aren't."

I'd never wanted to be good. I knew love and goodness were impossible for me. First, for my lack of a soul. Second, because I'd never learned to develop that weakness. Until she came along, and the word "good" was almost appealing to me if it granted me her. But Lily had a dark side. I saw her demons. If only she could allow herself to succumb to darkness so we could reign together in our madness.

Melissa's eyes glimmered at the view of the box locked on my office wall. She was too curious and wicked for her own good.

151

"Don't get me wrong, it's what I like about you." Her stare hit me with all her naughtiness as she inched toward me like a snake dancing for its prey. "You're merciless. Look at the way you punished me."

"You're being ridiculous, Melissa." I joined her in her macabre dance, looming closer. She wanted the monster? She'd get it.

"No, I get you, Radcliff." She bit her lower lip, trying to draw my attention to her. "I can make you forget about her."

She couldn't be forgotten. She had inked herself into my onyx black heart. Destiny had brought us together as my weakness, my only obstacle to the road of immortality. And now, I was hurting. She was my fatal poison. My eternal damnation. My own torture.

"We may share the same shadow and twisted mind, but…" I whispered to her ear, feeling the goose bumps spreading on her snake skin.

The corners of my mouth quirked up into a sinister smile that would give her nightmares.

My breath on her neck, I let my words penetrate her flesh. "You're a stray dog looking for attention, Melissa. You're the Lovers. Always seeking pleasure and to be loved. But no one will ever. You'll die alone. Your mother abandoned you because she couldn't love you. Your father beat you, treating you like useless crap, and you still stayed to win over an affection he would never give you. If I hadn't forced him earlier than planned to his grave, you would still be his slave. As for your choice of boyfriends, they just want your submission and your pussy, nothing more. A second choice—this is what you are and ever will be, and this is all your fault."

I then engulfed my eyes into the sadistic green of hers. Melissa's expression twitched, and her eyes would have watered if she actually had something else than a selfish heart.

"Get to know your place," I articulated.

"You're right." She managed a forced smile with trembling lips, but her hands locked into a fist. *Interesting.* "This was misplaced. I just wanted to offer my help. I should get back to work."

Melissa left, and I remained alone in the peacefulness of the void of the blackness.

The countdown had started, but my aching black heart called Lily's name.

Chapter 19

Lily

In Paris, the elements fought a battle of their own. The rain was pouring with sorrow. The storm was building with hatred. The light was being swallowed up by the apocalyptic clouds.

I had run like a madwoman to my uncle's place, slamming on the door with my fist until the neighbors screamed at me that he wasn't there. I had gone to my old maid's bedroom in Paris to drop my luggage—which contained my perfume and half of my clothes, since I had left the manor in haste. I had called my uncle. He didn't pick up.

And now, with a hammering heart that bled into each breath I took, I was waiting in the hall of our building, turning in circles countless times, ignoring my messy reflection on the broken mirror.

Eugene would come back. He had to. I called him once more. And again. Again, until the rings stopped and Eugene picked up, ending my misery.

"Uncle." I swallowed my wrath, managing it by locking my hand into a fist and digging my nails inside my palm. "Where are you?"

"I'm with the Carmins. Why does—"

I hung up and slammed the entrance door right open. I coursed through the rain, matching its fury and pain with my own. I didn't care about the cars splashing out on me, nor about their angry honking when I went through a red light or the gossip of passers-by who took me for ill. At that moment, nothing else mattered but the truth.

I was wet with madness, soaked to my feet when I arrived at the Carmins' villa—or, more exactly, that imposing display of luxury. I rang the bell of their fucking pristine white royal gate countless times. I'd even climb it if I had to. I darted my eyes at the camera on top, locking them with whoever was on the other side.

The gate opened, and I barged across the cobblestones to invite myself inside their mansion, dirtying their marble hospital-like floor. My eyes wandered on each side; their castle was way too big for one man and a stealer of talent.

"Can I help—" The valet at the entrance started to speak, but I made up my mind and rushed up the stairs facing me. He couldn't stop me. "Miss, you can't!"

Each of my steps was determined, fed with betrayal. I passed through the corridor with its red carpet and the heads of the Carmins as statues, along with pictures of Christian and his achievements. I paced that megalomaniac hallway until the end, remembering where his office was.

"Miss! Please! Miss!" the valet screamed after me through the tiny elevator leading him upstairs.

I slammed the door open and thundered into his office like a bad omen disrupting their peace. My uncle was sitting on a regal golden couch with the biggest smile on his face, a cup of tea in his hand. My nostrils flared, seeing how happy he looked.

"Lily, I can't believe you're here, darling!" Eugene exclaimed with all his cowardice. "You're gonna catch a cold. You're wet."

I'll burn each of you.

I dug my nails deeper into my palm until my blood almost dripped on their pristine floor. My stomach clenched with the burning force of my restraint as my scorching glare hit Christian's. He was seated in his red office chair like a treacherous king—one that sent his own people to die for him, building an empire of misery.

He displayed his business smile as white as his floor, rising from his seat. "Lily, such a pleasure."

Adonis arrived from another room, probably at the sound of my name. His gaze traveled from my head to my toes, his eyebrows slanting inward. "You're here, and you're…"

I was a mess.

They all gazed intently at me as if I was the crazy witch that needed to be interned.

"Miss, I—" The nonathletic valet finally caught me but stopped his chase at the view of Christian. "I'm sorry, sir. I tried to stop her from disturbing you."

"It's fine." Christian dismissed the valet with a wave of his hand. "Lily is like family."

Asshole.

I dug my nails into my fists harder, squaring my shoulders. The valet excused himself, and my eyes gunned between Christian and my uncle.

"Lily, are you okay?" My uncle pretended to worry about my silence.

"I know what you did." My lips twisted in repulsion, and anger rose in me like a tide that couldn't be tempered. "You stole mom's perfume!"

My uncle's face went ghostly white in a catatonic stupor, and his eyes widened in alarm. He didn't blink but gulped cowardly, processing the fact I had exposed his lies.

"How could you!" I screamed, making the windows shake and my howl echo across the room like the shriek of a fury. "How could you betray her like that?"

My uncle remained mute with regret, the world probably collapsing at his feet at this precise moment.

"Lily, what are you—" Adonis tried to interfere.

"Ask your father!" I yelled at him. "No. 27 is my mother's perfume. My uncle sold it to your father when she died. You're all fucking liars!"

Christian laughed. "Nonsense. When did you hear something like—"

"I'm so sorry, my Lily," my uncle pleaded, tears wetting the corners of his eyes.

Christian's face tightened. He became rigid, shooting a warning glare at my uncle. Adonis was lost, his eyes swiveling between me and his father.

"It was the only way," my uncle lied.

"There is always a way, Uncle! Just like the way you chose to abandon me. You betrayed her! My mother would have never wanted that. Why did you do this? You never cared for any of us," I bit out, tears like a hot torrent of lava spreading on my cheeks. "At the sisters', you left. You never came to pick me up. You never loved me." I pressed my lips together, trying to stop those wretched tears. He didn't deserve them. "And you never loved Mom. I hate you!"

All my demons came out.

The ones that were eating me alive for years.

I gathered them today, choosing to not be against them but with them in a battle that would destroy my soul.

"Lily, please…" My uncle's lips trembled before he hid them

with his hand. A tear of regret dropped on his cheek, but it was already too late.

"Come on." Christian advanced toward me, readjusting his suit as if I was a business deal he wanted to win. "I'm sure there is no need to yell. We can all come up with an agreement and talk like civilized adults."

The way he smiled at me with confidence and the lack of respect for my family sent a shiver creeping down my spine. He had used my weak uncle and stolen my legacy. He was a gifted manipulator portraying himself in a blessed light while he was a pervert. A narcissist.

I picked up a spicy scent that burned and tingled me. I wiggled my nose, but the smell sneaked into my cells. I took a step back, on the verge of tripping under the chills of fear scouring over me. My mouth opened in a silent scream. "No, it can't be—"

I hit the porcelain vase from behind me, which shattered on the ground.

Odors never lied.

It all rushed back and hit me at full speed.

Black pepper and cinnamon.

"You." Each fiber of my body shook, the hair on my skin rising with alert. "It was you at the club."

Christian's withering eyes darkened, but his creepy smile remained polite. "I don't know what you're talking about, Lily."

"You tried to—" I wanted to vomit at that smell, the nausea making my stomach spin. "You tried to fuck me. You knew it was me. That's why Adonis said you had a bruise on your face. You didn't get beaten up. It's because Radcliff stopped you that day. He did that to you and—"

Radcliff's revenge.

Radcliff started punishing Christian for what he did to me that night at the club. Radcliff knew all along. He had entered a war for me. He wanted to protect me. From him. Because he knew I couldn't fight this battle on my own after what Christian tried to do to me.

"Lily, why are you saying this?" Adonis's jaw went slack. His father had manipulated him too—he had no clue.

"Your father is a liar and a rapist! He goes to a club to fuck young women, and he's—"

"Let's talk in private, Lily. You're certainly not feeling well for having such a wild and vivid imagination." Christian's voice pretended to be sweet and paternal, but it was laced with venom.

I glared at the hand he held out to me with disgust.

"No." I switched my attention back to Adonis. "You have to believe me, Adonis! I'm telling the truth. Your father isn't who you think he is."

"Why would I believe you?" Adonis's eyes sharpened with anger. "After what I saw you doing to Radcliff and the way you've been behaving lately... Now you're accusing my dad of such things? What's the matter with you?"

"Adonis..." I wailed.

"I told you to stay away from him. Look what he did to you! You're siding with the evil side of the story." Adonis gulped, girding himself with superiority. "But it's not too late. We can help you if you—"

"No, you don't—" I shut my mouth, eying the three of them. I was done. They wanted me to believe I had lost my sanity. It was all pointless.

My uncle was mute, staring in the middle of nowhere, and even if he did believe me, he was too much of a coward to speak against Carmin. He had sided with him from the start.

I narrowed my eyes at Christian with a promise. "You'll pay for it. No. 27 is mine. The truth will come out."

I would put the final ending on the reign of Christian.

I stormed out of this soulless living room, my heart filled with hatred.

"Lily! Come back!" My uncle yelled after me.

I locked myself inside the small elevator, pulling the iron grille, fully decided on leaving that place behind. Right before the elevator departed, Christian was ambling toward me.

His eyes danced wickedly, and a demonic smile curved on his lips.

His mask had fallen, and he thought he had won.

***

Being in my old *chambre de bonne* felt ghostly. Depressive. Lonely.

It felt more exactly like I had been pulled awake from a dream to land inside a frigid nightmare with no light.

The only remaining part of Ravencliff Manor was inside my luggage—my notebook of recipes, or some would say spells, and my creation. I hadn't even smelled it since I arrived at my place, consumed by the rotten scents around me, letting them wrap me into a cloud of misery.

Sitting on the balcony of the roof, even the view that once was beautiful and magical was now blurred, as if all hope had been erased from the landscape. My uncle knocking at my doorstep for the ninth time seemed like a distant memory. It was too late for forgiveness. The sound of his persistent knocks vanished, and the silence filled my inside gloominess once more.

Radcliff and I didn't feel over. We would never be. But the impossibility of being together made my heart ache and transformed the color of my soul into a ghastly white world.

I'd have to get back on my feet, eventually. I squared my shoulders, sat straighter, and lifted my head, locking my eyes on the horizon. A last tear dropped under my expressionless face, and each of my features closed. I'd present my perfume to the world. The pain was momentary, but a masterpiece was forever.

My phone rang, interrupting my thoughts. It was an unknown number. I furrowed my brows. I wasn't in the mood to talk, but a gut feeling in me spellbound my fingers into accepting the call.

"Lily?" the woman's voice called. My nostrils immediately flared. I could smell the illusion of her green notes of mint and galbanum. "This is Melissa."

"What do you want?" I exhaled, already cursing my damn gut.

"Something happened to Radcliff at the club."

My heart stopped pounding, and my whole body stiffened. "W-What?"

"He asked for you. I'm calling you because despite everything, I care for him. Look—" She took a deep breath. "He said something like not doing an aphrodisiac. I don't know what happened between you or what the fuck you did together, but you destroyed him, Lily. He needs you. If you love him, you'll come save him."

My eyes widened in fear. My heart cracked into tiny pieces that drew me toward Radcliff. Hundreds of questions spiraled through my mind. "Save him from? Why isn't he doing the aphrodisiac? Is he okay? I—"

"Just come, Lily. I have no time to explain." She paused. "Or don't. I don't care. After all, I'm doing this for him."

She hung up.

I went through my phone's contacts and let out an absurd laugh. I didn't even have Radcliff's phone number—how could I have hoped to win his soul?

I climbed up to my window and grabbed my keys decisively.

There was no other choice.

I'd always be there for Radcliff, no matter the outcome.

Chapter 20

LILY

"It's here!" I screamed to the taxi driver pulling in front of Club 7.

I rushed through the elite guests waiting eagerly in line in front of the entrance. The list was like none other I'd witnessed before. Politicians with shady reputations. Powerful figures who escaped judgment. Celebrities who had been subjected to scandal. Each of them was a sinner in Radcliff's eyes, which could only mean one thing.

Radcliff's plan was to make them pay.

Tonight.

I peeked at the invitations held in their hands while making my way to bypass them one by one. It didn't make sense. The invitations were gold, with bloodred handwriting promising a night of excess like they had never experienced before.

The aphrodisiac.

Was he launching it? Despite the many complaints of the crowd, I was mincing my way up to the imposing security guarding the door. Melissa was with them, making an announcement.

"The club is closed for the night, we're sorry." The guests revolted in sync, and Melissa gunned her eyes at them. "Your invitations are extended for tomorrow. We're experiencing a short delay for tonight's show."

"Melissa!" I pushed through the rest of the crowd, arriving next to her. "Where is Radcliff?"

She sighed, opening her arms to me and giving me a hand sign to join her. "Not here. Follow me."

We bypassed the main door through the secluded alley to arrive at a small iron gate at the back of the building. The place stank of trash and urine. With the badge around her neck, she unlocked the steel back door and wrenched it open.

We stepped inside, and the only noise coming from the club was Melissa's heels on the floor. It was deserted; not even the music was playing. Only the red spotlights danced wickedly in the main area, giving the vibe of a murder scene. The smell was vacant, chaotic.

My body tensed, a wave of acid welling up my stomach as we reached the corridor where the private rooms stood. "Where is he, Melissa?"

"He was in a meeting inside this room when—" Her chin shook, and she held the handle, struggling to articulate her next words. "He's—"

She didn't finish her sentence, and I screamed, the fear of losing him consuming all my cells, "I need to see him!"

"Prepare yourself, Lily." Her voice was laced with sorrow, and her mint scent was stronger than I'd ever smelled.

"Open the door!" I shrieked.

My heart jumped to my throat when her badge unlocked the room. The smell of ashes and death poisoned my nose in a draft. I stepped inside the place, holding the nightmares of what could have happened, letting the corrupted air engulf me into its wickedness. In the midst of the darkness of the room, there was only a spark of red.

"Radcliff?"

Nothing but the whisper of demons warned me to step back, and a wave of cold froze me in place. I had entered the lair of a spider that would trap me in its web, and with this thought, I felt a sudden stab of terror in my gut.

And then, the door closed.

Chaos swallowed me whole.

And I screamed.

❧

Meanwhile…

Radcliff

"Are you entirely sure about this?" Hugo asked, his brows knitting together in disagreement, as if I was known to change my mind and second-guess my decisions—especially because of someone else's worries.

I rolled my tarot card between my fingers, the slide of it calming my nerves. "That was always the plan."

"It's just—" Hugo looked at his feet for a moment. Hesitation wasn't in his usual temper; he was impulsive. Too heated like the fire sign that he was. "Lily. You lost her because of this. Is it truly worth it to—"

"I haven't lost her." My hand locked into a fist, crushing my card with the motion.

My Adam's apple bobbed, and when I opened my palm, the destroyed card fell on the floor of my office. Perhaps I was delusional. Perhaps I had lost her. Everything came with a price, after all. Especially in hell.

"I've always been on your side Rad, but this time, I…" Hugo gulped, cowardice sparkling in his eyes.

"You either speak now, or you get back to work, Hugo." My voice was laced with bitterness, matching the red hellfire traveling through my veins.

"I'm out this time, Rad. I'm sorry, but this has gone too far. I can't witness that." Hugo squared his shoulders, but his voice was tinged with hesitation and fear. "I thought Lily would make you see there was more to life. I understand revenge, but this is inhuman. You're taking away their free will—we don't even know what this thing could do. Nothing good will come out of it. You're stuck in your past while Lily is offering you the future. I mean, you had everything a man could dream of, and you've become… You've become exactly what you fought against."

A monster.

Fury sprang to my core, liberating my hellions bound in my Tartarus. Life wasn't meant to be wasted; I couldn't be content with what any man aspires to.

I would take their free will just as once upon a wretched time, they took mine.

If I had been just a man, and not a beast, I could have loved.

If my father hadn't carved my face and made me a demon, I would have ruled the heavens.

If I hadn't grown in the shadows but learned how to feel and love, I would have been happy and capable of feelings.

If I hadn't saved her, I wouldn't feel like I had *lost*.

But all of those actions made me. It was too late for salvation. Free will was a lie. We were bound to the rules of society. Money. Other beings. All of those people waiting outside were sinners, and I'd make their masks drop. I'd bring to life their true impulses and darkest cravings, and I'd be there to watch humanity fall apart. They'd become the murderers, rapists, perverts, psychopaths, and sociopaths hiding underneath their doses of luxury and lies.

I was the Devil in a quest for immortality.

A man without a soul, whose heart had awoken and learned how to beat in a black aching color.

I thought Lily would be my death, but she had only killed my heart.

"Are you done?" I gritted my teeth, narrowing my eyes at Hugo. "If yes, you can leave now."

Hugo nodded, backing away, until he looked back at me as if he was holding wisdom inside of him. "You know, I believe she could really love you for who you truly are. I'm not talking about that mask you're wearing and hiding underneath. The mask of someone who doesn't feel or believe a thing because, Radcliff, someone devoid of a heart would not seek to save the next victims of these sinners. I know there is good in you, just like I know you'd never have to change for her. Just to heal, Rad. It's your choice. I hope you'll get what you want. I always looked out to you as an example."

Hugo left, and I remained stupidly fixed on the door, the weight of his words stuck on my fucking jaw. I didn't even notice that my hands had balled into fists, and when I took sight of my reflection in the windows sneering at me, I liberated my wrath eating me from the inside.

I smashed away all the objects on my desk in one destructive move. They all crashed on the floor in a shrieking noise similar to stained glass windows in a cursed church that had been shattered by creatures of the night. I seized the desk in a roar and knocked it down like an altar that broke in two.

Breathing like an animal, I sensed liquid sliding down my forehead. I passed a finger over my cheek, only to see black blood on my thumb. My scar had reopened like the stitched-up monster that I was. I scowled at the scene and stepped on the broken objects on the floor, shattering them even more.

Let the chaos enter.

"Radcliff!" Melissa appeared with the best timing like usual. She sprinted to my office, her heels crushing the pieces of broken glass. "Holy shit…" She gasped, finally taking notice of the redoing of my office: an altar for the damned.

"Get. Out." I was about to burst into flames.

"It's Lily," she said, out of breath. "She's here."

My eyes opened, alert. "What?"

"Yeah, she's gone crazy. She asked everyone to leave at the entrance, yelling crazy things! She thinks you're up to some evil plan and—"

"Where is she?" I commanded, my brain unable to function properly from the moment I heard her name.

"I locked her inside of room one. I didn't know what to do with her. She was unstoppable!"

I rushed to the security cameras and watched the first room. Lily was here. Inside, in the dark and curling on herself in a corner. No. No. No.

"What the fuck did you do!" I roared. She was scared of the dark, and she was surrounded by it. This was a nightmare for her. "Let's go."

Like a madman, I bolted down the stairs, not thinking twice. Lily was locked inside. Even if she wanted to tear apart my business or, for what it's worth, kill me, it wouldn't matter. I'd gladly give her the torch or the knife to do so if it meant I'd get to see her again. She needed me. I couldn't fail her.

Melissa ran behind me, not fast enough, as I arrived in front of the room.

"Open it!" I ordered her.

Melissa scanned her card, and I rushed inside the soundproof room, finally able to call my flower goddess out. "Lily!"

All black.

There was no sign of her.

"What did you—"

The door locked behind me. In a flash, the bitter taste of betrayal angered me. Melissa must have switched the cameras.

Lily was still stuck in one of those rooms, and I was—

"Fuck!" I hit the metallic—and impenetrable—door like a maniac. Blood spread on my knuckles, but I continued, even if I knew I wouldn't be able to break it. I'd had them built. The only escape was with the badge.

Stopping momentarily, my demons on the prowl, I heard a whistle.

Fuck.

The aphrodisiac was getting poured inside those rooms.

Chapter 21

Radcliff

A wild storm rushed through my core.

An evil plague took hold of my limbs.

Bolts of fire blazed over my corpse.

I was a bloodred monster, like a vampire awakening from his tomb in a thirst for blood.

Damn it. This wasn't good. I was about to become my worst self. The aphrodisiac infused like venom, hungering the monster inside of me. I had spent all my living time managing my impulses, and now they'd get freed without any turning back.

I grunted, falling to the ground, my whole body aching for a release, submitting to my human flesh. My vision reddened, calling out for blood, to take each of their pitiful lives. My cock was as hard as a rock, and I gripped onto whatever I could, resisting the addiction—no, the need—to touch myself and end my torment.

"Lily!" I screamed my whole guts out.

Initially, I was yelling to warn her. Save her. But now, I was calling her name so I could take her and use her savagely to pleasure myself. I'd enslave her to me, tighten her in the ropes at my mercy so I'd kiss, slap, lick her until I was satiated. I'd devour her until our last breaths, so we'd die in a flood of pleasure.

My hand stroked my length through my pants, having a mind of its own, and I was getting off on this idea. Gasping and moaning, the waves of pleasure hit me the hardest. I needed to find Lily. To fuck her. *Yes.* Oh fucking—

"Fuck!" I was reduced to a slave. And worse, I wouldn't save her. I would destroy her until none of her remained if she came here. I'd even be capable of killing Lily by breaking her—I wanted to have her in my arms, gripping her with all my strength to feel her heart beating for me. I was her nemesis in that battle, and she needed to be away from me.

The Death.

I managed to slap my hand away from my cock and punched the ground instead until I got off by inflicting pain on myself. But bleeding me out wouldn't hold the monster any longer. It just wasn't enough.

Blood. Blood. Blood.

My mind asked for it.

Pain. Pain. Pain.

My vision blurred in the midst of my oblivion, or was it the afterlife? I squinted my eyes to see the door slamming open and closing.

Lily.

My dick pulsed at the thought. Someone was in that room. A cruel and sinister laugh twisted my mouth. A prey had come to play.

"Lily? Is that you?" I ripped my shirt open, my diamond cuffs and buttons slipping onto the floor. How good she'd look licking and sucking the gemstones with that sweet mouth of hers. Drops of sweat slid down my forehead; I was a blazing sauna.

Come to me.

She wore a gas mask like the ones people had during the war and a fancy red dress as she approached me. Was this role play? I laughed wickedly, working on my zipper. *No, go away. Escape.* My mind went into delirium, and I resisted the urge to free my hardness and drive deep into her like a fucking sexual predator.

I shut my eyes, but my mind was corrupted by the illusion of Lily in all her beauty and fierceness. A queen in a silky black dress, sitting on a throne of bones. Parting her legs for me and offering me her sweet pussy. Flames rising and—

"Think again, Radcliff," the feminine voice whispered and echoed in my head.

I slammed my eyes open and sharpened them. She, whoever that was, was squatting in front of me, stroking my knees. I tried to see her eyes behind the gas mask, but instead, I saw the color of her green, envious soul. "Melissa... what did you do?"

Another wave of pleasure transcended me, and I hit the ground, my cock throbbing with madness. Orgasming was a necessity. The more I resisted it, the more it grew, ascending me into the most ruthless of monsters until it tore me apart. *Better me than Lily.*

"You always underestimated me, Radcliff..." She caressed my aching face, and that single touch made me want to mount something. "All I ever wanted from you was your affection. But you always rejected me."

"Lily," I groaned, my cock ready to jerk off, my palm stroking it through my pants. "Where is she? With who—"

"Her?" She laughed. A laugh so cruel, it was like a melody of damnation to my ears. "She'll soon be with Christian—remember him?"

"What?" My roar echoed in the room as I instinctively grabbed Melissa's neck and slammed her against the wall—whether it was the spell of the aphrodisiac or I actually wanted to kill her, I couldn't be sure.

"I called him." She lowered her two dress straps. "I helped him plan all of this. Switching the cameras. The trap. The revenge."

"How did you know?" I hit the wall next to her and dug my nails into my skin, trying to scar myself so I would fight the need to fuck. *Unless I kill her?* She deserved it, after all.

"About the aphrodisiac?" She laughed again. "I heard you and her fighting at the manor when I was on my way to make you change your mind about that job of mine. I knew you couldn't be with her just for her pretty eyes. She had to be useful to you. I wondered for so long what you found in her... now, I know. That sorceress built you a weapon."

"I—" I was too weak to continue to speak and hit the floor once more. My palms stroked my hardness. I was at the mercy of my darker needs, stroking and stroking. "How much? How much did you put?"

"All of it."

Idiot.

She would kill us both.

A drop was enough. But now, the effects would be fatal.

Lily... She can't stay here.

Melissa put her gas mask away before crouching on top of me. "Look at you now. So weak and needy. You'll beg to have me just like I always wanted you. And tonight, I'll not be the second choice."

She parted her lips, and I furrowed my brows, unable to move any other part of my body unless I gave myself what I wanted. A fucking release. "Christian… he doesn't love you. Stop this. I won't give you what you—"

She shushed me with her fingers on my lips and rubbed her body against mine, lifting her dress. My hand grabbed her waist on instinct, my grip so tight I could break her ribs. She liked that.

A bolt of red lust destroyed my cells when I looked up at her. Her face had switched to the perfect one of Lily's. The illusion that it was her became stronger, and soon, I'd succumb to madness. It was just a matter of seconds before I fucked and killed Melissa before ending my own life. Fuckkk—

"You treated me like shit, Radcliff. I'd have never betrayed you if you hadn't pushed my buttons. I was seeking your forgiveness, but because of her—" She grazed her nails over my skin. "I told you, we are the same."

I shut my eyes, wishing it'd erase the illusion of Lily on top of me so I could end this.

Her hand traveled to my zipper, and she added, "Selfish."

She kissed my neck, and my hand fisted her hair.

"Possessive," she cursed, rubbing herself harder against me.

"Open your eyes, Radcliff." Even her voice seemed to be different. She became more like Lily every second. Unless… unless it was truly her?

My eyes opened, and hope surged through my veins. "Lily…"

My flower goddess had the sweetest smile on her face. Melissa had disappeared. My Lily was here. She wasn't in danger anymore. I cupped her jaw and kissed her senseless, liberating my urges. My tongue entered her mouth, and I would possess her until we'd bleed each other.

But the way she tasted, like a mayhem of wickedness, wasn't her.

Kissing her should have liberated my demons and my weak humanity, but it didn't.

I felt nothing, only the void.

You could lie with your senses but not with someone's soul.

I broke the kiss and the illusion with it. I threw Melissa away, even if my vision wanted me to believe I had thrown Lily against the wall. But Lily wasn't here. She was still in danger.

Another wave of the aphrodisiac hit me as I squirmed on the floor away from her. I stroked myself harder and harder like an animal. I had fallen into my own trap. *No one else will save her if I don't escape. Fight it. Fight it.* It was my fucking fault.

"Radcliff… I need you," Melissa whispered, her legs parted as she touched herself.

Her card. My hormones pulsed in need as my eyes darted to every corner of the room, searching for the card that would allow me to exit. Melissa had it in her hand. I crawled to her, my eyes stinging as if blood wanted to come out of them by dint of fighting my urges.

"Baby," she murmured, gripping my suit with her nails to draw me to her.

Fight it. My jaw tensed, and I towered over her. *Fight it.* Her body began to shake, her fingers trying to rake my back.

"I love you," she cried out. Love—that's why she did all this. Melissa couldn't love properly. She was a narcissist. "I love you so much, it kills me!"

I seized the opportunity of her weakness to grab the card and escape from her. But my time was up. My orgasm was building up, gnawing at me from the inside out, and very soon it was going to explode if I didn't feed my demons.

Don't be weak. No human could resist it. It was impossible. It engulfed you in your deeper sins and cravings. It was like releasing all evil on Earth, just as Pandora's box did.

Just like Melissa, I couldn't love properly. I wasn't conditioned to it. Didn't know how to. And if by a miracle I came to feel it, it wouldn't be the same way as other people.

I'd been hell bound with evil from the start.

But love could deliver me, as the priestess once said.

"You should leave." I shot a last glance at Melissa, who drowned her pleasure in tears. She had bound love with pain and misery; that was the way she had learned to feel it. The only way she could love. She was a victim of herself.

I rushed to the door. Fell to the floor. Rose up. Fell again. It was a fight between heart and body. The cards had said Lily would be my death. But perhaps it was the death of something else. The one of my father's soul that had remained inside of me, haunting me. I'd be reborn, just like a phoenix rose up from his ashes.

The Devil's Corpse.

The voodoo.

My father.

I had never been human.

I had been raised in hell by true evil and conditioned to darkness.

And if someone could beat hell, it was me.

Because hell… Hell was the way I loved.

Lily, I'm coming for you.

Chapter 22

LILY

Paradise.

The moment the first note of the spray wafted past my nostrils in a heavenly draft, a horde of goose bumps had traveled the length of my body, and my cells had burgeoned with blooms of pleasure. It smelled floral, like a delicious euphoria, or more likely, an exotic and sensual elixir.

The scents enveloped me completely, rocking me in a world of their own. A world where I had fallen from creator to victim. In this world, reality no longer mattered; only their exquisite manipulation did.

This is so good.

So wicked.

Yet, so wrong.

Alone in the red room, I rolled on the floor, on the verge of succumbing to madness. I was beaming, feeling a hungry pulse beating inside my belly. Oh no. The effects of the aphrodisiac were coming, and instead of preventing this, I was giving up to my dementia in a laugh of pure bliss.

I'm sorry.

I raked my hand through my hair, lifting it into a bun, feeling the rays of a scorching sun on my skin. I parted my lips, thirsty, my eyes desperately searching for the drop of water that would deliver me from this infernal heat.

I heard my breath echoing in my ears, and closing my eyes, I could feel the fragrance settling on every part of me. The notes were coming to life, to the point where I felt the strong arms of a ghost circling me from behind.

It set me aflame, the heat slowly consuming my senses so I wouldn't be a master of my fate any longer. My eyebrows furrowed, and I dropped my hair down my back. Still under the embrace of the aphrodisiac, I thought of Radcliff.

His name was a spell, triggering a wetness that pooled between my thighs and a clenching stomach.

"Radcliff," I moaned, the room now smelling of a kiss on the lips. A devouring, heated kiss. The kind that takes your soul away and colors your heart in a rainbow. A true-love kiss.

I rolled my hips, feeling the need to feel love deeper and its power. All of my senses multiplied, and opening my eyes again, I took sight of the reddish colors of the scents dancing around in a spray that looked like fairy dust blessing this moment.

"Lily," a voice echoed.

There was a shadow in front of me, and at the thought, my clit pulsed. Radcliff? No, it couldn't be him. But why did it look like him? Another pulse heated me, and I held on to the wall behind me, biting my lip as hard as I could.

The pain aroused me and didn't stop the wetness between my thighs. On the contrary, my breasts ached in response with the need to be touched. I curved my back, offering them to— *Fuck.*

Another wave hit me, and in a gasp, I managed to speak out loud. "Who's here?"

A tie fell on the floor. A red rose one. The shadow inched closer, his face too blurry to perceive any form. "You look just like her. You always did."

"Who?" A tear of pleasure fell on my cheek as my breathing became short and sharp.

"Just the color of your hair is different."

Where did that voice come from?

"Radcliff…" I called in a whisper for help, my hand traveling to my inner thighs.

Writhing on the ground, I firmly squeezed my legs together to prevent my hand from going through so I wouldn't touch myself. An anxious feeling crept through my spine, conjuring the enchantment for a rapid second.

"He won't come. You're all mine now."

Adonis?

I squinted at the man unbuttoning his shirt. He looked like Adonis. The azure eyes. The golden hair. My nose was already drugged with the heavy smells around me, so I couldn't smell him. I was blind.

The man squatted in front of me with a sharp pristine smile. "It's okay, *princess.*"

Seized with terror, I tried to slip away from him, but I hit the wall.

Christian. *No.*

My body begged in agony, and I curved myself on the floor,

feeling another wave pulsing on my clit. A tear rolled down, and I feared for the worst.

"Radcliff…" I didn't even know if I was wailing his name out loud or if it was all in my head. I needed him, but I was the slave to my weapon, and soon, I'd be begging the man that I hated to end my suffering.

"Sshh, Nicole…" Christian caressed my cheek and crouched next to me. "Stop resisting me."

Nicole… That was my mom's name.

"Why—" A new bolt of pleasure hit me, and I cried out, curving my hands into fists. "My mother," I mumbled.

"If only you hadn't rejected me, everything would have been as it should have, Nicole."

Why was he still calling me by my mother's name? What did he mean? I couldn't reply, unable to speak the words. The aphrodisiac had eclipsed all thoughts from my mind, and Christian's fingers caressed my collarbone to descend on the valley between my breasts.

"I loved you, Nicole," he breathed. "Now, I hate you, fucking whore."

Unable to rise up from the floor, I remained completely at his mercy. As he towered over me, Christian became my fantasy, taking the shape and traits of Radcliff. The burning wave hit me harder, and I smiled, welcoming it.

"Radcliff…" I called.

He grabbed my breast on top of the fabric of my dress in a move that was hard, devoid of tenderness and respect. My heart leaped to my throat, about to combust. He wasn't him. He didn't feel like him. Radcliff had made love to me the only way he knew how. It was surely violent. Possessive. Hard. But every single touch of his worshipped me, creating a firework of sparks deep in my core.

Carmin didn't; he was using me, exposing me as an object he wanted to serve himself on.

But the scent… The scent betrayed all of my other senses.

I clenched my pelvis forward with carnal need. Christian was on top of me and crushed his lips on mine, our teeth clashing. My brain and heart revolted, but my body was too weak to push him away. I surrendered to it, knowing it was all too late. I'd lost everything. The image of my mother slapped through my mind, and tears spread like a hot torrent.

His hands moved to my soaked panties, and the pleasure was unbearable. It tingled in my flesh, to the point that my vision blurred and I could only see a white glow calling me in the middle of the depths.

His touch left my body in a fraction of a second. Perhaps it was all in my brain? I rolled onto my belly, lifting my butt cheeks up shamelessly so my fingers would meet my clit, and another wave of pleasure hit me. A moan crashed into me, and I tried to keep my pace in check, or soon my orgasm would crush me in a thunder.

My cheek hit the cold floor, and hearing incomprehensible mumbles from afar, I peered to my side. Wait, where was Christian? There was no sign of him. Through my buzzing ears, I heard someone calling my name.

"Radcliff…" I whispered, stroking myself harder, like a bandmaster playing the fatal moment in a dramatic partition. I didn't mind if I came in the middle of the room.

My eyelids fluttered, and I fought to squint in front of me. Two shadows were fighting. One was on the floor, covered in a beautiful red liquid. *Blood.* I licked my lips, feeling my eyes doubling in size under the realization: Christian was bleeding on the floor.

I rocked my hips harder, not caring that my knees would be bruised, and parted my mouth. I could see only the back of the other shadow, but I knew he had come. My hellish monster. My phantom savior. My Radcliff. I inserted a finger inside me, then another, and laughed at the pleasure scouring me.

Radcliff grabbed Christian by the throat to lift him up and aimed his punch right in the middle of his face before smashing him against the wall. *Yes. Just like that.* My arousal climbed, facing that violence and justice. Seeing Christian worthless, his face disfigured with blood, made me smile. *Kill him.* Radcliff's wrath in his eyes when he looked back at me was the most beautiful landscape. I wanted to feed on his darkness. *Oh my—*

One last stroke overpowered me, sending me into a place further away than heaven or hell, and my orgasm crushed me whole in ecstasy. I exploded into a laugh so wicked like the witch I was, accepting my whole madness. *My heaven is in hell.* Perhaps because it was where I belonged? I wasn't only sweet Lily. Something dark had flourished inside of me the day I—

"Lily…" Radcliff's voice rescued me from my demons before I sank to a point where there was no turning back.

I was surrendering to my darkness, the aphrodisiac bringing out the worst of me.

But Radcliff led me back to the light.

"Radcliff?" I felt my strength draining and my focus disappearing as his black, imposing shadow came to me.

He swooped me into his arms, carrying me in his godly embrace. "You…" His lips moved, but I didn't catch the rest of his words until he said, "…safe."

The light. We advanced to it. It felt like flying. Radcliff stopped on his way, and he and Christian seemed to talk, but I couldn't hear them. It was as if a bomb had exploded in my ears, and their voices were far away, blurred by a thud.

"…it'll hurt," I heard Radcliff finish his discourse. "See you in hell."

I think Carmin pleaded.

The last thing I saw was a lighter in Radcliff's hand and a sharp Machiavellian grin on his face.

Then, a flame.

Then, the flame went away, and the room turned into fire.

Diabolic flames rose inside the club, tearing down the walls. The smell of smoke and burning invaded my nose. The fire tinted the room in charcoal black, marking this place of debauchery as a vestige of the underworld before it collapsed into ashes.

It was the death.

Radcliff carried me through the flames as if we were immune, and we left this chaotic place. On the outside, sirens cried out in the middle of the starless sky, and the effect of the aphrodisiac slowly drifted out from me.

Radcliff dropped me delicately on the floor, brushing my hair away from my face with a tender touch. "I'm sorry."

"Don't go," I begged, a tear trailing to my cheek.

"You're a part of me, Lily. I'll always be with you." *But not physically.* I had learned how Radcliff could twist his words into hiding the full truth. "You're my *soul* mate, but I can't—"

You can't offer me your soul because you believe you have none.

"Your heart is enough," I whispered, the sound of the sirens getting closer.

"It's rotten, and dark, and ugly. You deserve more." He brushed my face, his eyes roaming over each of my features. They were aching with a tortured pain. He was blaming himself, probably experiencing for the first time in a very long time the feelings of *hurt* and *loss.* "I was wrong… You are my strength."

He inched forward to me, his lips approaching mine, a few inches from touching. "Twentieth of January."

His birthday.

He placed a fairy-tale kiss on my lips.

Not the kind that would awaken me and give me my forever happily ever after.

But the kind that was a goodbye, bewitching me in a deep sleep.

Chapter 23

Lily

It smelled of white.

White, like the afterlife and the nothingness.

A scent of clean and chemical that left no place for colors, as emotionless as the blank pages of a book.

"Lily? Look, she's awake!" I recognized my uncle's smell— paper journal with an amber note.

My eyes fluttered open, and the cold and merciless white became blurry. I shifted my head, feeling my uncle's hand holding mine. My vision adjusted to distinguish two shadows that were bent on top of me—my uncle, who had a tear in the corner of his eye, and Hugo, who let out the brightest beaming smile.

"Nice to see you back, *doudou*." Hugo grinned. I tried to lift myself into a sitting position, but he interrupted me, his hand on my shoulder keeping me in place. "You're fine. But take it easy."

"I'm so sorry, Lily. I know you can't forgive me, but I—" My uncle pleaded, clutching his grip on my hand with a grip so tight it'd cut my blood from flowing. "I can't lose you like I lost your mother."

I pulled my hand away from him and sat my back against my pillow, despite Hugo's instructions—who this time didn't question me. My heart felt empty and heavy, the flashbacks of what had happened at the club scrolling through my mind.

The fire. Radcliff's club. It all burned out.

The aphrodisiac. It disappeared.

Christian. He was dead.

I even wondered if Adonis knew about his father. We had all lost something that night and left behind a part of ourselves. Forever.

"Where is Radcliff?" I locked my hard stare on Hugo, erasing those images of chaos in my mind.

"He's fine, but…" Hugo readjusted the pillow behind me before giving me a thin smile that meant he was hiding something. "You need to focus on you, *doudou*, okay?"

"No," I quipped back. "I need to see him."

"Lily, you need to think—"

"Uncle," I cut him off with all the bitterness inside my soul. "You have nothing to say. You lost that right."

My uncle quietened, his head bowing to the floor before he took a step back.

"It's not possible." Hugo crossed his arms.

"If you don't bring me to the manor, I'll go on my own." I was determined, unbound by the rules. I wouldn't stay in that emotionless white smell any longer. "And knowing Radcliff, that's something he wouldn't want me to do."

"Just like he knew you'd say that." Hugo snorted, shaking his head in disbelief.

"Would you bring me, then?" Flames of hostility licked through me, my eyes not budging from him.

"Do I have a choice?" he complained.

"No." My lips curved into a proud smile.

"I'll get the doctors to get you out, and I'll drive you." Hugo then eyed both my uncle and me. "I'll let the two of you... resolve your evident issues."

Hugo took his leave, and the silence filled the room. My uncle didn't even dare to look at me anymore. His gaze was frozen to the ground, his fingers intertwining with each other. His lips moved like he was whispering something to himself, but he made no sound. He looked like he was senile, a madman lost in his world.

Eugene had been a coward and an unworthy uncle. His heart couldn't love me or anyone because he couldn't love himself. He was weak but not evil.

"Why did you give away Mom's perfume?" I broke the silence, swallowing my fresh swell of anger toward him. "And no more lies. I know she would have never wanted that."

"I don't know." He fell on the chair, his eyes lost in the room, like he was finally seeing the truth that clouded his vision all this time. "I was a failure. Your mom had always been better than me... And I thought..." His chin shook. "Perhaps I thought I could steal her future. Her talent. I was a screwup who crawled under debts. I wanted to show everyone I could have a higher social status. That I could be the talented one. People made fun of me, you know? They called me *the rat* because they said I was useless and ugly. I got bullied a lot in my childhood. I used to come back every evening with bruises on my face, torn clothes, and they were stealing my things. Once, they even threw me in the gutter... I was the laughingstock of everyone except for your mother. She always stood up for me. She was so strong... And that's how I repaid her."

He brought his hand to his nose, and the tears of regret

consumed him. "Before your mother died, she had become paranoid with all the substances she was taking, saying they would all want her perfume. She looked scared, but I wasn't there for her. She made me promise, whatever happened, to keep No. 27 in the family. She wanted this to be your legacy, but I—"

His mouth trembled, tears flooding him with the burden of his betrayal. "I can't… This is too hard."

"Continue," I ordered him, my heart palpitating. "Please, Uncle. You owe me the truth."

"I betrayed her," he admitted. "Carmin offered me prestige and a huge deal of money for it. He was the first one to treat me like *a friend* and not like *a rat*. He told me that I could prove them all wrong. You see, we grew up in the same school. Christian always had a crush on your mother. I never understood why she was turning him down—to me, he was all I ever wanted to be. He was the rich, popular one, and he offered me the chance to not be an outsider anymore.

"I was too weak, and I accepted his offer… I can't look at myself in the mirror anymore. She trusted me to take care of you, and I couldn't even do that. I'm a failure… A coward." He leaned forward, twisting his body, his tears exploding in a new wave. "I'm an impostor, it's true, but… I love you, Lily, and I loved Nicole. I'm so sorry."

My uncle's demons had caught up to him, the regrets of his mistakes washing over him. My heart broke, witnessing his past that had left irreversible consequences, but I remained cold as stone. He had sold out his family for his glory. He'd made his own misery.

And most importantly, I had learned Christian knew my whole family from their childhood. How could he have done this to us? He had fooled everyone, his death hiding the darkness of the truth.

I'd give my uncle a chance to have his redemption, because his weakness did not condemn him to hell. "Will you do everything you can to get Mom's perfume back?"

"Yes." His eyes shone with a new hope. "Yes, I'll do anything. I want to be better for you. I want to be the uncle you deserve, and perhaps one day you could forgive me?"

"I don't think I will, ever." I felt the bitter aftertaste of the lies hanging from my mouth. A part of me already did, but I wanted him to be in pain. The same as I had been. I wanted to torture his soul until my mother's memory was avenged.

"It's okay, I understand." He wiped away the tears. "It doesn't change anything. You've always been my hope, and you've opened my eyes. I'll prove it to you, Lily. I'll make things right."

"I'm not sure if I should believe you." I hit him with the coldest stare, digging my nails into my palms, ignoring the pain aching my heart.

My uncle rose from his seat, curving his body in defeat. "People can change, Lily. For love, we can."

The media had invaded Paris.

They fed on Christian's death like vultures. Even in his death, he was the center of attention. Him, and the announcement of his extremely new rich successor, Adonis, who finally got what he wanted. The empire of his father—or what was remaining of it. His legacy was cursed.

Club 7 was now a vestige from the past, in ruins, and Radcliff was a phantom. He stayed in the darkness, his name not even mentioned in this tragedy.

The road to Ravencliff Manor was empty and hazy, as if some evil plague had wiped everything out, and we were entering a land erased from the maps. Hugo and I were deadly silent, focusing on our own shadows under jazz music.

The ocean was tormented, stormy, its waves crashing into the rocks with brutal force. The air was humid and somehow nostalgic. It smelled like sad endings and tears. We plunged into the forest that welcomed us into its macabre gloominess and advanced toward the imposing gate under the unwelcoming glare of the gargoyles. Mrs. Walton was closing the iron doors, and Mr. Walton carried some luggage to a small green car from the forties parked next to it.

They were leaving.

"We need to—"

"I know," Hugo cut me off, accelerating and drifting his sports car quickly to park in the middle of the mud.

I rushed out of the car and ran in the direction of the Waltons. "Wait!"

Both of them ignored my scream. I sprinted through the wild grass, using all my breath, and I arrived in front of Mrs. Walton, blocking her path to the car. She looked at me with wide eyes as if I was the craziest of the two of us.

"Is Radcliff here? Lead me to him, please," I implored her, hoping she'd reopen the gates.

"Excuse me, who are you?" she said.

Mrs. Walton spoke.

I took a step back, and my jaw dropped open. Phantom ants scattered across my arms, and I whirled around to look at Hugo. He seemed as confused as me with his eyebrows knitting inward.

My attention focused again on Mrs. Walton. "You spoke? How?"

"I don't understand." She gave me the brightest of smiles with benevolent eyes like those of a loving grandmother. "Are you lost?"

Hugo arrived next to me with a perplexed stare.

"The curse," he whispered. "It must have broken."

I took Mrs. Walton's hands, my heart slamming in my chest. "Please. Where is Radcliff?"

"There is no one by that name here, dear." She chuckled. "That house has been uninhabited for years since my mistress died jumping from the cliff. You must be mistaken."

Mrs. Walton passed in front of me, ambling to the car. Her husband was already waiting for her inside by the driver's seat, completely disinterested in what was happening around him.

"No, no, wait—" I rushed to hold her back, but Hugo held my wrist, stopping me from moving forward.

"She won't help you."

"Please, Mrs. Walton." I didn't listen to him and begged her with all my guts. "It's me, Lily. If you know something, you have to tell me. If you cared for his mother and for him, you need to help me."

She stopped and turned around slowly, her eyes boring into mine.

"You're free to visit. I believe the gentleman here has a key in his pocket?" She opened the passenger door of her car. "Who knows, you may find something rather interesting."

Her lips curved into a slight smile.

She knew.

She remembered.

"Let's go, my love," she said to her husband, entering her car. "It's time."

Hugo and I remained magnetized by the couple. Their car engine roared, and just like that, they left the manor like phantoms belonging to the past on the road to heaven.

"Did you also get the feeling they never truly existed?" Hugo asked, his stare locked on their green car, which was now just a black dot in the distance.

"They got their happy endings." They were proof that curses could be broken. I shot a glance at Hugo. "Now, let's find him. I believe you have the key?"

Hugo furrowed his brows, searching in his pocket before taking the key out of it. "Would you believe me if I told you I have no idea where this key came from?"

"Well." I raised an eyebrow. "Nothing surprises me anymore."

"Yeah, me neither."

Hugo opened the gates, which squeaked with a shrill noise, and I ran toward the manor, followed by the croaking of the ravens and the dead leaves flying in the path. Ivy had grown on the facade, giving the impression that the manor was abandoned and much older than I remembered.

I wrenched the dusty main door open, and a draft froze me in place. It felt like death, and dark, haunted spirits had just escaped from the hallway, finding their happy ending too. The manor was deadly and empty with no recognition that someone had once lived here. No furniture remained. It was as if Radcliff had never existed. Even the scent was different—it smelled only of dust and wet wood.

"What's all this?" I stepped inside, searching every corner for a sign of Radcliff. But everything was gone apart from the chandelier.

Hugo didn't reply. His face was completely closed off. He wasn't even shocked.

I confronted him, my lips twitching in an expression of disgust. "You knew he had left, didn't you? That's why you agreed to drive me here. Did you lie about the key too?"

"No, I still have no idea where that key came from, I swear," Hugo defended, raising his hands in a sign of innocence.

There was no need for him to reply about the rest. He had always been on Radcliff's side. I shook my head and bolted up the stairs to find anything that would lead me to Radcliff. He must have left something. The Devil had always played a game. Tricks. I just needed to find which hints he could have left me.

Radcliff could anticipate all my actions and read my soul. But I could also read him. I wrenched the door of his office open, thundering inside of it. Nothing. Then, I went to my old bedroom. Nothing.

I burst into every room with determination, but I ended up finding nothing.

Starting from scratch, I inhaled the decaying air of the hallway upstairs. I was about to give up when I noticed a detail that had escaped me until now. All the paintings of Dante's Inferno weren't here anymore. Only one painting still hung. The one of the portrait of the young boy. The one that was so beautiful but haunted.

I stopped in front of it, grazing the boy's face with my fingers. I lost myself in his eyes filled with pain and secrets. *What did you want to tell me, Radcliff? Was the boy you?* I readjusted the wobbly frame, putting it right, which wasn't quite like Radcliff's perfectionism.

An envelope dropped from the painting.

An envelope with my name written on it in black ink.

I knew it. I opened it eagerly, finding some documents inside. It was Radcliff's research that would hopefully help me get my mother's perfume back from Carmin. A beaming smile took over my face, and hope surged through my veins. I looked at the bottom of the envelope to see if there was anything else.

"What's this…"

My heart pounded in my throat.

I pulled out a card with one sentence.

You have to remember.

Goose bumps paralyzed my whole core at the view of the plant remaining at the bottom of the letter.

A purple flower bound in hell, whose posterior sepal formed the helmet of the lord of death.

The queen of all poisons.

The aconite.

I dropped the letter to the ground, a silent scream shattering my cells. Memories flashed through my mind in flashbacks, and I felt the earth opening below my feet.

"No, it can't be…"

How could I not know?

"What does it mean?" Hugo's voice echoed from behind me.

I crouched to the floor, my watering eyes locking on the portrait of the child.

"It was him," I cried out. "All those years, Hugo, my guardian angel had always been him."

Chapter 24

Lily

13 years ago

A cloud of steam escaped from my mouth.

Don't be scared, Lily.

My skin turned the color of blue hydrangeas with unstoppable shivers. My nightgown wasn't enough for the cold winter. Even the old tree in front of me screamed in agony. Its branches were like a dark monster who wanted to catch me and make me plummet to hell with him. The grass was wet. My feet were bare. The moonlight owned the night with a wicked smile that inspired only nightmares.

"It's okay, Lily… Nothing will happen." I curled my toes on the grass. "It's still better than the dungeon, right?"

At least I hadn't heard the silent screams of the phantoms of young girls. Tonight, Mother Anne hadn't locked me in the dungeon. She said I was too bad and that I should stay the whole night standing up in front of the ghost tree that looked like wandering specters to think about my behavior. If I sat or fell asleep, she would strip me and inflict much worse. I should never look behind me either. My hands were tied behind my back with a rope so I wouldn't flee.

Maybe I did deserve it? I did burn a Bible with my scented candle. In my defense, that was a mistake—one of the girls had startled me, coming at me with a broom and asking me to make it "fly" into the sky. To be honest, I liked that Bible. I'd used it as a notebook for my ideas.

The wind cried out in a shrill noise like a banshee.

Monsters were coming.

I focused on something else: the smells.

"Wet grass…" I took a deep breath. "Bark…" My nose frowned. "Smelly mint." Then, I picked up the last note, my eyes switching to the flowers near my feet. "Aconite."

I tried to kneel without falling backward and plucked out the flower to take it in the hollow of the palm of my hand. Mom always told me to stay away from that purple flower—it looked beautiful, but it was evil.

It was a deadly poison; that's why she called it *the queen of all poisons*. Its roots were lethal and could kill a human. If we ingested it, we would die in excruciating pain. It was fatal. I tightened my grip on the aconite until she gave me her venom. Just by touching her, I would feel her toxicity, and that's what I wanted right now.

Make me suffer.

End my torment.

A cracking noise echoed, and I let the crushed flower drop on the grass because of my leaping heart.

"Who is it?"

No one answered, but I heard footsteps, and a shadow loomed behind me.

"I didn't move," I defended myself, knowing that it'd change nothing. If they wanted to hurt me, they could.

I felt the touch of a stranger caressing my hand. My shoulders jumped to my ears in apprehension, a spider crawling up my back. But the touch was gentle and kind; I wasn't used to it. Most of the physical contact I'd had since Mom died was through fights. In the space of a breath, the knot on my wrists broke free and fell to the floor.

The air of freedom called to me in a note of vanilla and burnt wood. "Thank you. How did you—"

As I started turning around, the raw voice of the stranger left me frozen in place. "Don't turn around."

"It's you." I obeyed, my eyes locking on the spooky tree and my back still facing him. "It's you, isn't it?"

He didn't reply, but I knew my angel had come. He was a he. His smell didn't lie.

"How did you do it? Boys aren't allowed here. You'll have—"

"Stop," he warned. "They're coming."

In a draft, I no longer felt the presence of the boy, and I reeled around instinctively. *Shit.* My heart hammered. *Was this all in my head?* The lights of the sisters' rooms were switched on. Mother Anne was running to me, holding her lantern with a frown and wearing her nun's headdress that made her look like an old shrew. It was too late to tie me back—she'd seen me. The other sisters were joining her. I'd have to face the punishment.

"Silly girl! What did you do again? Did someone help you out?"

I shook my head.

"I saw someone! Don't lie to me!" Mother Anne screamed like the brat that she was, accompanied by her horde of thirsty hyenas. "Vincent will co—" She cleared her throat under the puzzled gaze of the sisters, finding her composure again. "I mean, the director will come here soon, and he won't be as clement as me if you don't speak the truth. Now."

I squared my shoulders, my eyes burning with witchcraft. "No." I would never betray him.

"Fine," she cackled, and circled her belt between her fingers like a boxer before a fight. "I'll get the truth out of you."

"No!" I shook my head, taking a few steps backward. "Please, don't do this."

"Hold your arms forward." She played with her belt like a wicked creature of the night. She was a vicious snake. A scary tarantula. "If you refuse, it'll be your pretty spoiled face."

"Not my face." My eyes opened wildly in fear, searching for any compassion in the eyes of the other sisters. I found none. "You can't take that away from me!"

"I will if you misbehave. Now, your arms," that sadist ordered.

The girls of the institute were spying on the scene through their windows, laughing and smiling. I gulped away my feelings and stretched my arms forward, a tear ready to fall. *Be strong, Lily.* Uncle would come to get me soon out of this place. I shut my eyes, dread twisting my guts.

The belt latched on.

My body shook, the sobs of fear coming in waves.

The belt slapped on my skin in a whipping nightmare.

It hit me—at least I believed it did, but why wasn't it hurting? Why was I not feeling anything?

Vanilla.

I opened my eyes under the familiar smell. The back of my guardian angel was facing me, hiding me in his protective shadow. I craned my neck. He was so tall and older. He was built like a man. A feeling of hope surged through me.

My guardian angel had come.

"Who are—" Mother Anne's voice went shrill, and everyone else remained mute.

"You shouldn't do that to a child. You're cruel," the boy warned in a placid voice that left no room for sympathy.

I leaned closer to him, my cheek grazing his black shirt. I hid behind his imposing size, finding comfort for the first time in a long time. The boy had gripped the belt into a fist, and he pulled down, causing Mother Anne to lose her grip.

My breath hitched at the sight of the blood descending from the belt. He was hurt. Red marks, like scars, scattered over him as fresh blood flew down his forearm. He had sacrificed himself for me, preventing me from receiving the blow, but he did.

"Get out of here, young man, before I call the police," that old tarantula yelled, but her voice was edged with fear. "Demon child!"

"It's him!" Men from afar came rushing to us, pointing fingers at my guardian angel. *Oh no.* "Sir, we found him!"

I threw myself against his back at the sight of the scary director, Mr. Vincent. He was taller than everyone else, a mountain of muscles, looking mad and terrifying. The girls said he was worse than Mother Anne. I thought he was the Father here, but I was wrong— he only remained in the shadows of the institute like a ghost. Those who had seen him had nightmares about him. He was terrifying. *What would he do to us?*

"Get out," I whispered to my angel. "You'll have problems. Please. Save yourself."

But he didn't listen, locking his hands into fists and raising his voice so he would awaken the anger of the gods and make the sky thunder.

"You think it makes you big in the eye of God to beat a child?" The boy was certainly educated in the way he spoke and stood like a regal prince. "You'll not last one day in hell."

"Get him out!" Mother Anne screamed like the Queen of Hearts in *Alice in Wonderland*.

The men were getting closer to us, accompanied by the director, who had a ruthless walk and a terrifying half-smile. He was the effigy of power.

"Run!" I screamed to my angel. "Please, don't let them punish you!"

My guardian angel looked slightly to his side, showing me his profile hidden by his raven-dark hair that fell on his forehead. "*No one can take your soul away from you.* You have to remember that. No matter how much they try."

I nodded, my tears falling. His hand seized mine, and he gave me back my crushed aconite with a hint of a smile.

"Wait! What's your name?" I asked, but it was too late.

He gave himself voluntarily to the guards without fighting back. Even though the boy was imposing, he wasn't a man yet. Probably more of a teenager. The men grabbed him, and my guardian angel murmured something to the evil Mother Anne. The way her face twitched in response showed it wasn't a good omen for her. Then, they led him to the director as if he was a criminal.

"No, no! Don't do anything to him! He did nothing wrong!" I struggled to reach him with the sisters holding my arms, preventing me from joining my angel. I fought them, screaming like a crazy girl.

The cruel Vincent whispered something in his ear with hellish eyes, a tight grip on his arm. What was my angel going to suffer? Who was he? Probably a misunderstood outsider, just like me.

The boy looked back at me for the first time.

He was beautiful.

So beautiful to the point he made my heart stop.

His eyes were black with a touch of purple like a calla lily. He smirked in a dangerous and tormented way, as if he was untouched by the world. As if all the flames couldn't burn him.

The connection of our gazes gave me enough confidence to smile back, feeling empowered by his courage. *No one can take my soul away.* And just like that, we shared a secret. A silent agreement between us that no one could take away from us.

I mouthed the words *thank you*, locking the aconite deeper in my palms, under the stare of all the vultures who had watched this scene.

And I promised myself, the reign of Mother Anne would fall.

"Don't leave…" I murmured and felt my head spinning and my view blurring.

The last thing I saw was my angel disappearing in the shadows.

I fell on the grass and blacked out, burying that memory deep in my mind. So deep, I thought it was all a dream.

Since that day, I had never seen him ever again.

Or so I thought.

Chapter 25

LILY

Present

"It's been almost eight years since the Institute for Young Ladies burned down," I narrated to Hugo a chapter of my nightmares.

We stepped outside, the golden light dying away on the walls of Ravencliff Manor. The blizzard that had crept up in the forest was slowly fading. The solemn duskiness had found its peace; even the ghosts of the nearby graveyards were mute.

"It was some months after the director Vincent died," I continued my tale. "That fire… I remembered the flames rising like hell. The cries. The deaths. I escaped through the long corridors barefoot in my nightgown that night. I witnessed the doors shake and the people trapped inside their rooms screaming in horror. They were locked up without being able to get out. Nobody could save them—we didn't have enough time. Once outside, I saw some of the desperate ones jumping through their windows. It was suicidal. The whole thing was chaotic. Inhuman."

I had suppressed all the macabre memories of this place, but now everything came back to me like a whirlwind that ravaged me. My footsteps on the grass felt as if I was stepping on skeletons, and the pouring sunset had reddened with all the blood spread that night.

"How many survived?" Hugo finally said, coming out of his silence after learning the truth about my guardian angel.

"Me and some girls. Most of the sisters didn't make it." A pricking sensation shot up my spine. "We survived because our doors weren't locked. It was as if it was done on purpose."

"You think Radcliff did that?"

The air cut around us, stolen at the sound of Radcliff's name.

"I don't think Radcliff did that." My eyes locked firmly on Hugo's, and a burst of wind blew my hair. "I'm certain it was him. It could only be him."

He had burnt my place of nightmares and changed my life in so many ways.

He might belong to the darkness, but he'd helped me reach the light by enshrouding me in his black wings, defying the scorching heat of the sun burning his skin, and with arrows shot behind his back shedding all the blood in his body.

"After that night, I went to live with my uncle," I closed the chapter. "He wasn't parent material, and he let me down a lot, but he did his best."

"I'm sorry to hear that, *doudou*. But at least the one that bullied you, she died too that day. Justice has been served." Hugo smirked, doing his best to lighten the mood.

"Mother Anne?" I gulped, blood draining from my face. "She had another fate."

A fate I would rather forget.

"Hugo, do you know anything about Radcliff's father?" I changed the subject and paused, my eyes drawn straight to the greenhouse—or whatever was left of it.

The roof still hadn't been repaired. I was afraid of the carnage the ravens could have done inside, and a wave of protectiveness washed over me.

"I'm afraid not. He's always been very mysterious about this topic. You probably know more about him than anyone else." Hugo's eyes switched between me and the greenhouse. "You're his soul mate, after all."

"You believe that?" My cheeks turned crimson at the remembrance that Radcliff had used the exact same word to define us.

"You went through his church of scars to find his dusty heart. He's yours, and I've never seen Radcliff belong to anyone." Hugo chuckled. "You never hated him, even though he's probably the most hated man in France."

"You don't hate him." I raised a questioning eyebrow.

"Oh, I did… sometimes. He doesn't have an easy temper," he joked.

I smiled back and let my mind wander across every sharp edge of the manor. They pointed toward the sky like a seasoned sword. Ravencliff Manor truly was Radcliff's church of scars—from the windows in the form of stained glass to the gloominess of the unwelcoming place. It overlooked the terrible precipice, and one day, it'd collapse into the merciless ocean if the rock decided to let go.

There lived a cruel monster. Radcliff's father, who abused his own child. He was a villain, yet Radcliff's actions made him one too. But how come I couldn't condemn his darkness? Fourteen years ago, I'd seen the same darkness in—

"Something is on your mind, *doudou*."

"It's just…" I shook my head. "Never mind, it's nothing."

"You shouldn't hold everything inside. It's what Radcliff did, and it slowly destroyed his soul."

"The director, Vincent," I enunciated as one would summon a ghost. The wind rose up, probably fleeing away at this baleful name. "He looked like Radcliff. Terrifying. Tall. Imposing. Feared. It was like looking in a mirror."

Hugo's eyes widened. "You think that Vincent is—"

"His father, yes, and I hate myself for it. To compare them. To see the resemblance after everything he did to him. To—"

"Stop torturing yourself, *doudou*." Hugo's hand stroked my arm in an attempt to calm my nerves. "Radcliff has a darkness, but he's not him. He's just lost. He made a different choice by allowing himself to feel with you. You brought him back to the light."

"You don't understand," I dropped in a whisper. "He had to survive his father by becoming worse than him to beat him. And a part of it was because of me. Because he protected me. I'm his weakness, Hugo, which means I have the power to—"

"Plummet him into the darkness for good and make him become… him," he finished.

"Yes."

"But you also have the power to heal him."

"I'm not the ray of light everyone thinks I am." Remorse devoured me inside.

"You don't have to be." He grinned with all his reckless confidence. "I'll wait for you by the car."

I nodded, and we parted ways. I strolled one last time around the garden. The fountain had gone silent, butterflies circling around it. As for the greenhouse, I thought it'd be a graveyard where rotten flowers had given their last blooms, but I was wrong.

Turning the handle, I entered into its magical supremacy. Ivy had grown on the windows like a ribbon surrounding it like a sacred gift. The flowers had bloomed beautifully in a landscape of colors and infused into a spring scent. The earth wasn't dry and decaying anymore. It was wild. Hopeful. Luminous.

I walked toward the hole in the middle where the Devil's Corpse used to stand like a queen. The hole was deep, as if it was a tunnel to hell itself. I crouched in front of it, my fingers grazing the earth. "Someone dug you up."

There were a few broken petals left on the ground which would disappear with time, and a few roots which were only a fragment of her splendor.

The Devil's Corpse had been unearthed for a reason.

He searched for something.

My lips drew into a smile.

Radcliff had taken the seed.

If I could grow life in the underworld and bloom the heart of its soulless king, then, perhaps, he could revive her in her afterlife.

Chapter 26

LILY

Day 1

Dear Radcliff,

We weren't coincidence.
We were destined, our story engraved in stone.
Written with the blood and feather of an angel,
We wage wars on the demons of fate in the pit of hell.
Our souls were damned but bloomed with obsession.

You thought I was bound to heaven, but you were the one born with wings.

My guardian angel.

You're wherever I am,

And I know now, you'll never leave my side. You never did.

For the others, you're the monster who hid in the shadows.

To me, you're the savior who protected me from your own monster. Your father.

Your skin had burnt because of me,

For the punishment you suffered for siding with the witch.

You saw my darkness.

I saw your light.

We can't escape each other.

I know where to go now.

To my Elysian fields.

"Where do you want to go?" Hugo's voice called out to me from the car.

"Grasse," I spoke with determination, my eyes set on my letter burning with the flames of the lighter.

The words turned into ashes, until none of it remained on earth.

Chapter 27

Lily

Day 23

Dear Radcliff,

You were my spring, planting your darkness into my wounds and gardening my heart that is now a fortress of stone on a dry, wintery fall.

But I'm blooming.

In Grasse with Hugo, I'm telling the story of what happens when the witch of the fairy tale wins—if only we could win together. I've captured your diamond heart with me. You thought *it was a black, worthless rock, but I'll immortalize it into the shape of my perfume bottle.*

Each scent smells of you.

Perhaps, because you're here with me, in each of my breaths and steps?

You're the one my guards on the flower fields are talking with through their headsets.

You're the one they take the pictures of me for.

You're the one who asked them to watch over me.

But you don't let me reach you—except during my dreams. You're mastering that illusion. I know you'll reappear when the time is right. After all, the Devil is the most tenacious of all, just like our connection shatters all the physical boundaries.

Together, we're pure madness.

But we are us.

Imperfect and magical.

Your flower goddess.

"Is it another one of your letters for Radcliff?" Hugo asked from behind me, snapping me out of my reading. "You don't have an address."

No one knew where Radcliff was—not even Hugo—but that wouldn't stop me.

"I don't need an address." I lit the lighter and burned the corner of my letter, watching the flames dissipate over my words.

I waited for the letter to turn black and for the flames to scorch me to throw the rest of my letter into the fireplace.

Soon, only smoke and ashes would remain, and I hoped it would go to hell to reach its recipient. Its ruler.

"Why are you doing this, then?" Hugo packed away the papers for the launch of my perfume and sat beside me on the couch of my Mediterranean villa. "Is it some kind of therapy?"

My eyes were empty, stuck on the fireplace. "I'm burning the letters because I'm hoping the hellfire will bring my words to hell. To Radcliff."

It was more of a spell.

An incantation.

Might as well give my nickname right and try out witchcraft.

"You must think I'm crazy, right?" I snorted, meeting Hugo's stare.

He had been a true ally for me the past month. We've made of my colorful, sunny house gifted by Radcliff, a perfume temple. The whole place was spacious enough, so we could work on the design and the marketing of my creation. Working occupied my mind so sadness wouldn't wash over me. Twice a week, he met me up here, in Grasse, making sure I wasn't missing anything over homemade tea inside my ceramic cups.

"Let's face it, you can't be crazier than Radcliff." Hugo gave me a cocky grin, and we both laughed.

It was nice to talk to someone. Truth was, I hated being alone even if I was in my definition of paradise. The house was beautiful with its lavender-and-citrus drapery, its forged cornices, mosaic elements, and tiled stone walls. And most importantly, I only had to open my wooden shutters to discover the majestic landscape of my flower fields and let the sliding windows open so that the floral notes would infuse my nose in a blessed draft.

Sometimes, I even heard the barks of Cerba and smelled the scent of the Devil's Corpse, but they were all gone with the Devil.

"We all have a part of madness inside us, and I believe that's good. The world isn't boring this way." Hugo positioned his elbow against the cerulean couch and leaned over me. "You know I'll always be here for you, right? Even if you're in need of more than my business services."

My eyes widened, and he grinned in response, his eyes sparkling with mischief.

"I'm joking. Don't get any ideas. No offense, but you're not my style." He rose up from the couch. "I know you miss him, but what I meant is that you can count on me. Not because Radcliff asked me to." *Obviously, he did.* "But because we're friends, *doudou.*"

"Thank you, Hugo." I escorted him toward the exit. "You're always welcome here if the city ever gets too loud."

"I'll keep that in mind, but it's never too loud for me." He crossed the arched doorstep, entering his playboy sports car. "By the way, what name did you choose for the perfume?"

"Obsession." I didn't hesitate, and a beam tilted my features. "Obsession by the Flower Queen. The brand name is a tribute to my mother."

Obsession was what brought Radcliff and me together and what tore us apart.

A cocktail of love so magical and deadly.

A perfume that had paid the price for his creation.

"Love it." Hugo cranked the engine of his car until it roared. "We got a lot to do together, *doudou.* The first step is the launch of Obsession—"

"The second, to get No. 27 back."

Chapter 28

LILY

Day 67

Dear Radcliff,

The world's alive again, but you're not in it.
The world's colorful, but you went back to the dark.
Don't worry, I'm not waiting for you. I'm living each day
like death is chasing after me. But I have a chase of my own.
Eternity.
Obsession will overcome the barriers of time, you'll see.
Just like us.

I'm not giving up on you. Stop ignoring me, Radcliff. Stop hiding. I need you.

We are bound to—

A cracking noise startled me, and a splash of ink spread at the end of my word.

"Damn it!" I cursed, dropping my pen on my letter sheet.

I glanced up to see above the flowering buds from where I was lying on my field of flowers, wondering who was here. I inspected the life around me. The butterflies flew. The bees were working. And near the apple tree a few meters away, the doe had returned.

Our eyes locked from afar in the same mimicry. She was holding a red apple inside her mouth. I rose up, dusting away the herbs on my white linen dress, and squinted my eyes back to her under the heat of the sun. It had tanned my skin to a golden hue, and its rays now burned my shoulders, so much so that I longed for the shadow.

The doe dropped the apple as if she knew I craved to use the shadow by the apple tree and departed to her enchanted forest. The guards hadn't seen anything, walking the hundreds of steps around my field.

I chased after the doe, running through the flowers, holding the long length of my dress to the side. I interpreted her presence like a sign from the Devil. The air brushed my hair into a magical breeze, and facing the tree, I scooped down to seize the apple only to see that it wasn't an apple.

My lips parted, a drop of heat descending along my forehead to loosen onto the fruit.

It was a pomegranate.

I craned my neck to peer at the red fruits hanging from the tree branches.

A pomegranate tree.

I tiptoed to pick another fruit, a smile hanging on my lips. I believed in magic. In signs. In Radcliff. He had said this fruit would bind us together, and I believed him.

I would munch the fruit willingly again despite the warning of the tale. I would let its juice spill over me in a reminiscence of the promise Radcliff and I made.

And most certainly, I would not lose faith.

"Eternity," I whispered.

That's what awaited us.

"Miss Bellerose?" The voice of a man interrupted me from behind, and I let the pomegranate roll onto the grass.

The marine smell invaded my nostrils with sea notes and seaweed. *LaMouette*. I reeled around to face him with his badly shaved beard, little glasses, and grayish hair.

"I'm here on Mr. Radcliff's behalf. He instructed me to deliver this to you," he continued, handing me a velvet box that he held preciously.

I grabbed it with a frown and a pounding heart. "Radcliff's timing is as always—" I smiled at LaMouette blanketed by the shade of the tree. "Uncanny. It makes you wonder if he's doing it on purpose." As if he had eyes everywhere and an intuition that was beyond our comprehension.

"Timing is always right." His lips curled into a thin line. "However, sometimes it brings us what we need, not what we expect."

Inhaling the spring air around me, I unpacked the box, and the reflection of the jewel inside blinded me with its brilliance reflecting on the sun. I recognized it immediately. "Is that the diamond I had chosen?"

LaMouette nodded, and I grazed the necklace with sparkling eyes. My diamond heart was untouched, enclosed by vines in white gold that circled it with micro blooms of lilies and calla lilies—the details were so small and precise. Radcliff had instructed this to be handmade for me. Around the diamond, there were tiny crystals, like particles hanging on the vines that looked like stars in the Milky Way.

"It's so bright and luminous." *Magic.*

"Because it reflects all the light it absorbs. The slightest flash of light forms a spark. This necklace glows in the complete dark," LaMouette chuckled. "Even though the complete dark doesn't truly exist."

My eyes widened—Radcliff did that because of my fear of the dark. On the hook of the necklace, there was engraved: "To my light which sparkles in my darkness."

"It's beautiful. He thought of everything and—" I looked up, and LaMouette was already leaving. "Wait! Do you know where Radcliff is?"

LaMouette stopped in the flower field, his gaze observing nature. "If you look closely at the necklace, you'll have your answer. Have a beautiful, glorious day, Miss Lily."

He left with a last smile, being as cryptic as the man whose life remained a mystery to all.

My gaze fell on the diamond, and it felt like I was holding Radcliff's heart in my hands. A breeze blew; the spirits had spoken in their turn. The message was clear.

Radcliff was with me.

For light and dark cannot live without each other.

Neither can exist without the other, just like us.

Chapter 29

Lily

"Congratulations again for the event, and thank you for your time, Miss Bellerose. Unless I should call you Mrs....?"

"It's Miss—I'm not married. But you can call me Lily." I gave the interviewer a last smile to conclude the interview. "It's been a pleasure."

The young journalist bowed his head, and I drifted away to the outside courtyard of the particularly Parisian hotel, otherwise known as a grand town house. I inhaled deeply, my tight sparkling dress with inlaid flowers giving me no room to breathe.

Hugo had surpassed himself for the launch of Obsession. My eyes and my nose marveled. Everything was perfect. The whole event smelled of floral happiness and cheerful colors. The garden was intimate, engulfed by renaissance architectural walls. Ivy climbed them, alongside some garlands of lights like fireflies sparkling in the twilight. A variety of celebrities were invited, from influencers to prestigious newspapers, thanks to Hugo and Patrick DeLange's elite list.

It was a dream come true. I hid below the stone arch, spying on my guests talking near the appetizers, tasting flower-flavored treats, and indulging in activities such as a photo booth or smelling the strips of Obsession.

"Your mother would be proud of you." My uncle appeared from behind me, a rose ice cream in his hand. "You should be the center of the attention, not hiding in a corner."

"I'm not hiding. I'm—" *supervising.* I swallowed my last word, a shy smile slanting on my lips. That was truly a Radcliff thing to say. "I did some interviews, but it's all very consuming to finally be… seen."

"Well, you deserve to be seen. Look what you've accomplished." His eyes flickered, locking on the bouquet of lilies of the valley at the entrance. "Her favorite flowers. Do you know why she named you after them?"

My uncle was trying. He had invited old colleagues and acquaintances of my mom to attend the launch, and for once, he wasn't trying to steal the spotlight—just eating all the buffet.

"Because it's a symbol of happiness and purity. I know the story, Uncle." My mother wasn't entirely right about me.

"No, that's not the real story." My uncle chortled.

"What?"

"Her favorite flowers were the lilies," he continued. "Until you. When you were just a baby, you came out of your cradle and plucked out a lily of the valley that your mother planted in the garden. When she discovered what you did, she got so scared… She was crying and yelling."

"Why?" The hair on my skin raised. I'd never heard this story before.

"Because the lily of the valley is very poisonous. You had ingested the plant, Lily. You had eaten all the little white bells. Well, it's a common thing for babies to eat a bit of everything and to—"

"Uncle, get to the point," I hurried him, my heart thumping wildly in my chest.

"You should have died or been hurt severely, my Lily, but you didn't. You were smiling as if nothing happened. It was a miracle." My uncle reached for my arm that he'd struck, his smile tinted with emotions. "Since that day, your mother had an obsession with that flower. She always put its scent in her perfumes. You were her flower queen. She called you Lily because she believed you were magical and that nothing could ever get to you, just like that plant. You'd be able to face adversity and defend yourself with beauty and strength."

I felt like I had been hit by lightning.

I had been bound to hell from the start by making a deal with the poison of a flower. It all started from there.

All my life, I thought my mother had named me after the lily of the valley because she wanted me to be sweet and plain Lily. But she had named me after it because she had seen the real me.

My light and my darkness.

My strength and my curse.

She saw my duality, that mix of beauty and poison.

"Thank you for that story, Uncle." I seized his hand in return, and just like that, my heart had forgiven him.

"We'll get No. 27 back, I promise you." With the palm of his hand, he wiped away his burgeoned tears. "Anyway, I should let you enjoy your night… but there is one more thing I wanted to tell you. I know you haven't forgiven me and that I've lost the right to be your uncle, but—"

"Tell me."

"Your nightingale will come back, and even if I think he's truly unworthy of you, he wouldn't want you to stop blooming in the meantime." My uncle gave me a light smile, pointing to the buffet. "I'll be here if you need me."

He left, and my brows furrowed. I knew this legend. The love story of a nightingale and the lily of the valley. It was inside my mother's journal.

Alone in the garden, the lily of the valley took affection of a nightingale that sang for her night after night. But one day, the nightingale had left her, thinking she was better off without him, that his singing didn't touch her soul, because she never showed him how she felt. She waited in vain for the nightingale to return. After some time, she grew so sad that she stopped blooming. One day, the nightingale returned, hearing her agony, and she flowered again, her happiness restored, just as the sun beams on a dense woodland night, penetrating the deepest gloom.

Radcliff was my nightingale. My lips curved into a thin smile, but it wasn't the moment to get emotional. Soon, I'd have a speech to make, and like my uncle said, he wouldn't want me to be sad on this day. I cleared my throat and ambled with confidence toward the crowd.

"Congratulations," a seductive voice interrupted me. It had the edge of someone important who knew his value.

I whirled around to face my interlocutor. "Thank you, I—"

My mouth hung open, and the words didn't come out.

I hadn't recognized him.

His arms were wrapped around the two women at his side— one blond model and one curvy brunette. His hair was now an ash blond, almost pristine white. His smile was sharp and vicious like a razor blade. His dress shirt was halfway open on a tanned body, as if he had spent a month on a yacht. An alcoholic drink was held in his hand, and he didn't smell of purple anymore but of carmine red and orange fire, a mix of apple cinnamon, cranberry, and poppies.

"Adonis?" A bad feeling crept down my spine.

"I got to admit, Lily…" He arched an eyebrow before snapping his dimples with another one of his sharp grins. "I was surprised to not have received an invitation."

"I—" There was nothing else to say. Adonis had lost his father, the same father that had stolen my legacy. "I thought given the actual circumstances you wouldn't have come."

He jerked his head backward with a laugh that drew all the attention to him. He then leaned back to me, pushing one of his women behind him as if she was nothing, his eyes shining with a mayhem of repressed emotions.

"Business is business, princess. I'm the head of Carmin—people expect me to be here." He then whispered to the blond girl by his side, "It would be a shame to not have your pretty face exposed in tomorrow's gossip journal, right, my dear?"

He wouldn't steal my spotlight. Nor his bimbo. The girl in question giggled, pretending to be shy, and I felt her spicy scent of fake luxury irritating my nostrils. *Unless it was that cat piss perfume of the last Carmin.*

Anyway, it was as if I never knew the real Adonis. For the sake of our friendship, I remembered the man that he used to be, hoping to bring out that side of him he'd erased for this asshole attitude.

"You know I have to get my mother's perfume back." I fixed my stare on him, determined. "It's not against you. I wish we could find a friendly way to deal with this. I still care about you, despite—"

"Lily." Adonis grinned with confidence.

He inched toward me, breaking the socially acceptable centimeters separating us. With one gesture of his hands, he ordered his dolls to vanish.

"Do what you should do." His voice brushed my ear the same way he did with the girl earlier. "But it would be a shame if another person had to die for that perfume."

Another person? Die? His words entered every one of my cells, paralyzing me on the floor. This was a threat. Did he know about what happened to Carmin at the club and the reason for his death?

Adonis chuckled, snapping a knife-sharp grin. "You look pale. Not that I mind—I always liked the color white on you."

I remained silent. Adonis had robbed me of the ability to speak. He snatched a lily of the valley from the bouquet, which he twirled between his fingers. "You know, just like the little white wedding bells of the *muguet*. It's funny—I always used to imagine myself as your groom, seeing that flower, but now…" He crushed the flower in his palm. "Now, I don't see anything. Enjoy your night, princess. I'll be watching."

Adonis passed in front of me in a draft that froze my heart, and I followed him with my eyes. He found his way back to his escorts and put his arms on their shoulders, acting like a spoiled child in an attempt to ruin my evening.

The voices around me turned blurry and distant, and I felt carried away by my thoughts, which detached me more and more from the event. Adonis's words were sinking me back into the dark.

Radcliff… My demons called out for help.

"*Doudou,*" Hugo interrupted my shipwreck, and my senses resurrected to life. "It's time for a speech. Are you okay?"

My nostrils flared, and I nodded. No one would take away my night. "Yes, I'm fine. Let's do this."

"I'll call everyone in."

Hugo did just that, acting as the host with enthusiasm. He took on the role to perfection. People listened, and all followed him into the small ballroom. It was a gilded room with tapestries and large royal windows.

Hugo stepped on the podium in the center and picked up the microphone. "And now, I'll introduce you to the incredible and

talented Lily Bellerose, who is none other than the owner of the
Flower Queen and the nose of Obsession. Lily Bellerose, everyone!"

The cameras were on me, dazzling me, and the applause began.
My legs yearned to flee, but I was stuck in the light. Hugo held out
his hand so I'd take his place. He gave me a reassuring smile, to which
I responded with a shy one. I seized my courage and stepped onto
the stage in front of the microphone.

"Hi, everyone, I'm Lily Bellerose, the creator of Obsession.
Thank you for coming here tonight. As you may have smelled with
the Obsession sample given to you, the perfume holds a unique
and personal story. One shaped by your memories and your own
conception of happiness. I'm inviting you all again to try it out."

Speaking about perfume gave me back my strength—it was
my universe. The guests all tried Obsession on their wrists, their
nostrils being filled with that elixir of love. Butterflies danced in my
belly at the sight of their faces—their expressions betraying surprise,
happiness, and amazement. They started to gossip heavily and snap
some more pictures.

"Obsession is inspired by love," I continued. "Love in its darkness and its light. Love in all its shapes. The ugly and the beautiful.
Heaven and hell. The strength and power of it. Obsession is dedi-
cated to my mother, whose passion and fire inspired me." My eyes
locked with the emotive ones of my uncle. "She taught me to never
give up on my dream, to be hopeful, and she was right."

I cleared my throat, denying the rush of emotions getting back
to me. "Obsession wouldn't have happened without the man who
showed me how—"

I stopped, my eyes lingering on the imposing shadow of a man
hidden in the back of the crowd. He wore an old-fashioned hat
and a long coat. Dressed in full black, his aura drew me to him like
a magnet. In the room, he erased everyone so that only he captured my attention. My heart pounded. It could only be him. A

phantom, invisible for those he didn't wish to appear to. Radcliff was my shadow watching over me in plain sight.

"He showed me how to express my whole self." A beaming smile took over my face, and all my dark feelings disappeared. "To be who I am without fear. We're all different. Perhaps we're all outsiders, but this perfume will make you love yourself for who you truly are. Be the goddess of today, the seductress of the night, or the princess of your kingdom. Or all of them together. Don't be limited to one category. Shine your glorious true self."

Applause rose and thundered as much as my galloping heart. I searched for Radcliff among the crowd, but he wasn't there anymore. He was leaving. Probably because I had seen him. I snapped my wide eyes at Hugo, who gave me a head sign that meant *don't you dare do that*, but I couldn't ignore the aching in my heart that needed answers.

"Thank you. I'll give the microphone back to Hugo—if you have any questions. I just—"

Seeing Radcliff disappear through the little courtyard, I jumped off the podium and let Hugo take over with an apologetic smile. I squeezed my way through the crowd, chasing after Radcliff.

My heart leaped with every breath I took, and adrenaline filled my whole body. Once outside, there was in the middle of the night a black limousine on the deserted royal bridge of Alexander III. I lifted my long dress and took off my heels, then left them on the ground.

Barefoot, I sprinted after Radcliff, who was advancing on the bridge, his coat forming the Devil's cape to join his ride back to hell. My bun came undone, and the locks of my hair fluttered through the breeze, a few still held up by the brooch he had gifted me.

"Radcliff!" I yelled after him, determined to not let him escape me, my heart necklace bouncing on my chest.

He opened the door of his limo and stepped inside it. *No.* I ran with all my might and quickly arrived at the car—the door had just closed with Radcliff inside. I banged on the glass of his window with all my madness.

The window rolled down, and our eyes met in a moment of eternity. My heart fell silent, peaceful, and the world calmed down. I yearned to kiss him, to throw myself into his arms for him to take me away into a world he had created for us.

Radcliff was just the way my dreams remembered. Beautiful and haunted. A dark king with a smell that lured me to him.

I had so many questions to ask him. So many things to say. But all that came up was "What are you gonna do now?"

"I always have a plan." A devilish half-smile slanted his mouth. Radcliff was, like always, on a quest. "Nothing like the aphrodisiac, I assure you."

"Something worse, perhaps?" I hinted by raising an eyebrow.

To that, he almost gave me a true, sincere smile.

"Magical, I would say," he replied, his voice laced with amusement. He then went serious. "You know I can't be good."

"And perhaps I wouldn't be with you if you were." I smiled.

Radcliff wasn't good nor evil. He was cruel to some. Merciless to others. Perfect to me. He had black needs and dangerous obsessions. He had a heart. A dark one that had gone through hell, cut with thorns. A soul that he had abandoned and needed to reconnect with.

A man, a beast, or a god—I wouldn't change anything about him, because neither part of him existed without the other.

"You're so beautiful, flower goddess. You're the only woman I ever looked at and will ever look at this way." His voice warmed my insides and bloomed my entire being.

"Which way?"

"The way where I feel the need to worship you. The way you brought to life my humanity, and the way you made me entirely yours." He stole my breath with his raw sincerity, exposing a vulnerability he never dared to show. "I wish you could come with me, but I'm trying to not be selfish with you after what I've put you through. I can't offer you what you deserve. You belong here. To the light. I'll always be your shadow."

You're more than that.

My heart was breaking through the tension. It all seemed like goodbyes. We were a part of each other, bound by something stronger than fate. But heaven and hell couldn't merge together; we both had a kingdom to rule. My place was here, for now. His wasn't.

All I knew was that the future was full of possibilities, and the impossible never scared us.

"I always thought I had a guardian angel. Truth was, I had the Devil behind my back."

"Forever," he promised.

"Radcliff," I mused with a trembling voice. "That day at the orphanage… Vincent, he was your father, wasn't he? Did you get that scar because of me? Because you helped me?" *Was I the reason you lost faith in humanity, as you once told me?*

My chin shook facing his tormented silence, and my eyes watered. I'd been the final reason he had stopped believing in humanity, the one that caused his status as a monster. The price he had paid for protecting me.

"I'll do anything for you, Lily. Especially the worst."

I let a tear roll down my cheek and pressed my lips together. I would show the same strength he had shown for me.

I squared my shoulders and cast a new curse on him. "You know, you said you can't run from the Devil. But, Radcliff, make no mistake, I'm a witch. I'll find you."

A fine line drew on his lips as dark mirth glittered on his purple calla lily eyes when he pulled up his window. "I'm counting on it."

Chapter 30

Lily

Lily Bellerose, the new perfumer you need to know.

Obsession, the perfume of Love.

How did she do it? The girl that revolutionized perfumery!

Obsession, the perfume that stole the spotlight from the giant Carmin!

I scrolled through the various headlines about my perfume and me, a huge beaming smile on my face. I hopped in place inside my little Parisian boutique, letting my joy run along with all my heart. The launch was a success, and I wouldn't stop until I created a myth around it. All the articles praised Obsession—it was a scent everyone wanted to smell, and people started asking questions about when the men's perfume would be out. A part of me was anxious about it, my inspiration lacking since Radcliff's departure.

I contemplated my accomplishment. The perfume bottles were stacked on beige shelves in the light of the crystal candlestick. I had put a touch of golden pink on the walls, with ivy and lilies of the valley climbing up on them. My name written in gold was visible from the street, thanks to the huge windows that formed an arch. The second step would be to launch the store in Grasse and compete with Carmin and its huge storefront.

"I'll see you tomorrow, Lily." Patrick waved at me, the bell chiming as he exited the store.

"Tell your family I say hi." I grabbed my keys, and I continued to put the Flower Queen shop in order.

I had hired Patrick to work in my boutique—after all, he loved the spotlight. Me, on the contrary, did not flourish as much as I thought. I had no more time to create—and worse, no desire to— perhaps because Radcliff occupied all of my thoughts, and life seemed colorless without him.

I closed the shop, and on the road to visit my uncle, I stopped at the florist to buy him a bouquet of lilies, daisies, and hyacinth to revive the smell of his apartment and brighten it. Today was the final step; all I needed was my uncle's complete testimony to have No. 27 back from Carmin. We'd been working with a lawyer referred by Hugo—needless to say, it was one of the sinners who'd worked for Radcliff.

I rushed through all five floors, being careful to not get my feet caught on the red carpet. I didn't want to hold grudges with Eugene. I chose love over hatred and believed he could better himself. No one was able to change, but we could all grow. Holding the bouquet tight to my heart, I stooped to pick up the key under the doormat.

I wrenched open the door and stepped inside. "Uncle, it's me! I bought you—"

I froze in place.

The bouquet crashed to the ground.

The rotten smell of corpses, of nightmares and tragedy, wafted up my nostrils.

A muffled buzz echoed in my ears.

I screamed with all the air in my lungs, writhing in pain. I broke into tears, my body ripping apart. My hands shook as I slumped against the door, powerless in front of the horror show.

My uncle was hanged in the middle of his living room.

A rope was tightened around his neck, his head bowing under the hardness of the grip. A chair was overturned on the floor, and his feet hung in the void. Uncle couldn't have killed himself. *No. No. No.* My tears were unstoppable, like a torrent breaking everything in its way.

There was a letter with my name on it, but I didn't dare go near to read it. The smell was too disgusting, rotten, the smell of death with—

My hair curled up in fear, my eyes crying my uncle's blood. I stepped back in terror, my hand covering my mouth to keep me from screaming again.

The 27 of Carmin.

The corpse of my uncle smelled of it.

This wasn't a suicide.

This was a murder.

✦

Panicking, I thundered inside Hugo's office with dried tears on my cheeks. I sprinted to him and collapsed in his arms, my whole body shaking under the shock.

"Lily, what happened?" Hugo's grip tightened around me as he held me closer to him.

"My uncle… He's—" A sob cut me off halfway, the words stuck in my jaw. "He's dead. I think Adonis did this to him."

I broke down again thinking about what Adonis had said at the launch. *It would be a shame if another person had to die for that perfume.* That was payback for his father. Adonis had nothing to lose compared to me.

My eyes plunged into Hugo's, seeking answers no one could give me. "He was my friend. My uncle's friend, and he did this to him. My uncle smelled of the No. 27. It wasn't a coincidence. Hugo, it's all my fault. I—"

"It's not your fault." Hugo erased one of my tears, keeping his stare hard. "I'm sorry about your uncle."

"I told him I would never forgive him. He died thinking I hate him, but I don't."

The memories of my uncle's corpse perfumed by my mom's stolen fragrance gave me nausea. I was fighting against these foul smells, a bitter aftertaste hanging in my throat and pain scorching my veins with hellfire.

"In the afterlife, he'll know the truth." Hugo stroked my arm in a friendly gesture and glanced away. "I'm sorry, I'm not good for this kind of situation. You know, feelings and all that."

"I—" I stopped midsentence, taking a step back from him before inhaling a deep breath. "I need help. I need him."

Radcliff was the only one who could deal with evil.

He was the only match to my chaos.

The one that'd go to war for me and save me from my torment.

"I don't know where Radcliff is, Lily… I've been looking for him, but he's nowhere to be found. He's untraceable." Hugo took a seat behind his desk and went through some of his papers. "If Radcliff doesn't want to be found, no one can."

"I can," I assured with a trembling chin. "I know I can."

I locked my hand into a fist, my nails digging into my palms. I'd deny my feelings once more, putting my pain inside a box because I would need my strength to get over this war. My heart was ripping apart, but the strings that held it had to hold on for a moment longer.

"Radcliff is looking for something in particular. I know him." I rested my palms on Hugo's desk, leaning my body against it. Hugo had always been loyal to Radcliff; maybe he was lying to me again. "Did you hear him talk about a legend? Somewhere secretive?"

Hugo thought this through, his eyes switching to every corner of his office, from its wooden shelf containing business books and family photos to a model boat with mini figures. "Not that I know of. I already tried to find him through the mines he owns."

"Mines?" My eyebrow rose, my eyes still locked on that model boat where the light of my diamond necklace was reflecting in a spark.

"Yes. He owns most of the precious stones on the market. But they're imported from everywhere; it's an impossible track to follow. I thought he would start over in a big city, but then again—"

"Wait." A thought came back to my mind, or more likely an oceanic smell at the sight of that boat. "Radcliff spoke to me one day about a legend of the three gates of hell."

Hugo frowned. "I've never heard of that."

"He mentioned one island being impossible to access, guarded by immense walls like some kind of volcano. Something with tides and a full moon. Erebas, or something like—"

"That fucker." Hugo jerked his head backward with a forced laugh before he went through his papers once more, this time searching for something in particular. "Why am I not fucking surprised."

"What? What happened?" My heartbeats increased in a rushed symphony, and the hair on my skin raised. The last few hours had been filled with gloom and chaos, and now a glimmer of hope was appearing, the appeal for revenge stitching the pieces of my heart.

"What happened, *doudou*, is that Radcliff and I meeting all those years ago wasn't pure chance. He already had a plan, and I was his pawn." He snorted, knocking his pen across the table. "I fell into the spider's trap like a fucking fly."

"What else could you expect from Radcliff? He may have had bad intentions at first, but you're his friend now," I defended the man who stole my soul, the one that could help me avenge my uncle's death.

"Oh, I'm not mad at him." He dropped the pen and gave me a wicked smile. "Well, *doudou*, I know where that island is."

"How? I don't understand!" I felt the madness possessing me.

"We're going back to my grandparents' natal home."

Chapter 31

Lily

The air smelled of death and ghastly spirits.

It was painful and somber like a wilted rose who had shed her last petal. Nonetheless, it held an omen of rebirth, a spark of light in this funeral.

I dropped my bouquet composed of purple anemones, yellow chrysanthemums, and white lilies on my uncle's tombstone, hoping the smells would lead him toward the heavenly afterlife.

The cemetery would be deserted if it wasn't for the occasional shrieking cries of the ravens posed on the trees overgrown with moss, whose branches had invaded the graves. In this place, nature had nurtured the spirits that men had abandoned, giving them a safe sanctuary. The weather was gloomy, the sun swallowed by the court of clouds. The wind was hot, like a draft sent from the underworld to take my uncle's soul with him.

"I hope you'll find peace, Uncle." I took a step back, my somber lace dress with black, burnt roses dragging on the wet ground like a macabre regal cloak, making me look like a corpse bride mourning her living fiancé.

Not many people had come to my uncle's burial. At least, not many people seemed to care about him; they were simply polite. No one shed a tear. Not even me. I had already shed a river of tears that could have filled a desert. I had none left.

I locked eyes with my bouquet, my face as hard and merciless as his tombstone. "I forgive you."

I shut my eyes for an instant to gather my strength before opening them and lifting my chin up. "We can leave now."

"Are you sure you want to do this now, *doudou*?"

My firestorm eyes met the concerned ones of Hugo and slid to his light beige suit and blue dress shirt. "I've noticed you didn't wear black. Why?"

"Personal beliefs." He shrugged before dwelling on the surroundings, frowning and curving his lips down with disapproval. "I believe we shouldn't mourn the dead with tears and pain but instead celebrate their departure as a new journey, by wishing them peace and by carrying the love we have for them in the abyss of our hearts. Death shouldn't be that macabre."

My lips curved into the slightest smile. "Maybe you're right."

After all, my uncle, as imperfect as he was, would have wanted my happiness, not my sorrow.

"And to answer your question, yes, I'm ready," I said from the bottom of my heart, with all its feelings and determination. "There is nothing left for me here right now."

"Your future is here," Hugo provoked me, knowing perfectly

I was more stubborn than he and Radcliff combined. "Everything you've accomplished, it's just the beginning."

It wasn't enough.

"My future is intertwined with Radcliff's." We'd been linked from the start, and life without him was dull and plain. "Even if we're doomed together."

My soul needed him for revenge.

My heart needed him for healing before it turned into ashes.

Without him, my obsession would decay, and my soul would wander in eternal oblivion.

Only he could resurrect the fire I was born with and help me grow into the infernal flower I chose to be.

"Do you want to change out of that wicked gothic dress first?"

"No." I embraced that new colorless part of me, that darkness and the nickname given to me.

That's what they made me.

Poisonous and cursed.

"Fine." Hugo's brows furrowed once more, a nerve in his jaw twitching. "Then I'll let the pilot know we're ready for departure."

I nodded, keeping my chin high. The wind blew, causing my dress to brush over the grass toward the little plain where the nature surrounding the cemetery started. My heart hammered, my nails digging into my palm.

I sent firebolts at the man dressed in a refined silver and carmine red suit from afar. A hundred meters or more separated us, yet I could smell his scent of treachery and luxury. With his white hair, Adonis displayed a knife-sharp grin with all his confidence and provocation.

"Lily. Follow me," instructed Hugo from afar, but I couldn't detach my gaze from Adonis.

He wasn't alone. Next to him was a colossal man, or more

like a war machine. Significantly taller than Adonis, he was at least two meters tall. A mountain of muscles, as if he was built of unbreakable stones. His neck, trapezius, backbones, and arms were of an inhuman size. His hands could crush you with a handshake. His lips were set to such an extent that they seemed stitched up together. His appearance sent a frozen chill scouring behind my back.

I had taken root in the ground, transforming myself into a marble statue that was cracking every second. Adonis chuckled, gesturing to his guard to walk behind him as he approached me. He held a lily of the valley in his hand, which he smelled.

"Uncle, don't pay attention to him. He's mine to deal with. He's mine to annihilate." I clenched my teeth, about to burst into him like a fury.

"Lily," Hugo warned again.

I clamped my nails deeper into my flesh and inhaled the air, my nostrils flaring. With heavy clamps, I ignored the acid burning my throat, and I decided to rejoin Hugo.

"Leaving so soon, princess!" Adonis yelled from afar, gaining my attention with a crazy laugh that echoed through the trees and blooms that had seemed to close off at his approach.

"*Doudou*," Hugo called out, shaking his head, his stare warning me to not listen to Adonis.

A burning wave consumed my core, and I faced Adonis and his madness, in thirst for his blood.

"I…" I whispered, the sound so low no one could hear it apart from the demons that were dancing around me.

My lips curved into a line that could send chills to the skeletons nearby. "Will…"

"Curse…" My voice was like a snake charming his prey.

"You…"

Until death tears us apart.

Blood flowed from my palm to seal this pact.

I eclipsed from my brain Adonis and his vile smiles as if he was only a shadow of the past and the object of my imagination, and ran toward Hugo, seized his hand, and jumped into an uncertain fate.

Chapter 32

Radcliff

Silence pervaded as intense as resilient fog.

In the darkness of the exotic jungle, nature was bleeding its heart.

The tropical foliage—from green aventurine to crimson death and coal black—dripped on the weedy ground and clung to any intruder who wanted to penetrate its hostile lands.

It was just as I remembered.

Chaotic and cursed.

In the land where the Devil's Corpse flourished, there was another legend.

Some said it was only folklore—but those who believed in magic and in history knew the truth.

I arrived back at the place that had given my father nightmares.

I crossed the valley of skulls carpeting the red sand to arrive at the wall of the cave, where tombs hung with a cross. The entrance had been condemned, with nailed pieces of wood and some words intending to frighten passers-by.

> ## "Do not seek passage or your soul you'll lose, and death will follow."

Good thing I didn't have one. That warning was sealed with black magic and blind faith so that anyone who entered would be swallowed up by its darkness.

A grin twisted my Machiavellian features.

I would reopen the mine he had closed.

Because inside of this island, there was what I coveted.

A curse that I'd break.

For her.

Chapter 33

Lily

"Hugo, what is that island exactly?" In the rush of events, I had blindly followed him, having not the slightest idea of what our final destination would be. Many questions hung on the tip of my tongue, but I refuted them, or else my heart would not take it. My emotions would be my strength; even if they consumed me, I would use them to get the justice my family deserved and to find the man who could stitch my heart together and heal it.

I held on to my seat, the helicopter shuddering as we entered turbulence, passing through an alley of stormy clouds. Bolts of lightning flashed in front of us in a landscape of apocalypse with no visibility.

"A land of bad omen," Hugo said through his headset. "Nobody dares to venture there from now on. Are you familiar with the Devil's Triangle?"

I nodded. It was the place where boats and planes had mysteriously disappeared. Another jolt made the helicopter shake, and lightning rumbled in front of us. We were blindly engulfed in the clouds, death chasing us in its shades of nocturnal gray.

"This island is worse. Previously, it served as a secret psychiatric asylum. They'd literally send anyone in there, from infamous prisoners to the sick or the nonguilty ones they wanted to exterminate in a quiet way. Since then, the population has reproduced and grown, even though everyone thought they'd die." Hugo turned to face me. "My grandparents were able to escape the island with my great-grandparents the day the Christians came to spread their religion, or more likely to kill our beliefs, and cleanse the island from its dark past. But that's not all—"

A light flashed, and I tightened my grip on the seat. We were losing altitude, descending at full speed on the black clouds.

"The history of horror and legends that surround this island is dark, *doudou*. You have to be insane to get back in there."

"Why did Radcliff come here, then?" I screamed into the headset as the helicopter continued to shake in its dive. *Why is he looking for this gate of hell?*

"I told you, he's insane." Hugo chuckled, having fun despite the fact that my heart was leaving my chest, the fear of death lurking on the corner. "For in the den of evil, there is always a hint of light."

And in a second, we crossed the barrier of darkness to arrive at the place we sought. The sun flared in crimson flames on an angry red sky.

It was as if the blood of the gods had been collected in a goblet to be spilled over the darkening sunset. The orange ray of lights, like hope trying to spark through this passionate sky, warmed up my face in a golden tone.

The blue of the ocean was restless and dreadful, as if its lost souls were trying to escape and take refuge on the island.

This was the unwelcoming kingdom of hell.

"This is the island," Hugo commented with a smirk. "Welcome to Erebus."

My hands stuck to the glass, frost forming around it. It was a warning to turn around before bad things happened. I leaned closer, my heart leaping in my throat and my breath creating a cloud of smoke on the glass.

This wasn't an island, no. This one was wicked, the air filled with tragedy and dark magic. I could hear from afar the whispers of the ghosts and their agony. This was the Devil's island, a red cliff standing with impenetrable walls preventing anyone from entering. The dry land of the volcano was like a well leading to hell. Its lava could erupt at any time and consume its wild forest, which seemed like the land of mythical creatures and prehistoric monsters that had vanished from the memory of Earth.

There was hardly any sand on this land—it was hidden in the hollows of the caves under the cliff—and it was crimson red, as if the land had been stained with weeping souls.

"Not what you were expecting, *doudou*?" Hugo turned his head over to me, giving me a grin, and my throat tightened in reply.

The helicopter circled around the island and came to a stop at the top, offering a view of a mine. My heart raced, being able to sense Radcliff's presence. My heartbeat was calling out to his in a melody that only he could hear.

"Hugo," I dropped in a whisper.

My gaze continued on the path, and emerging from the hostile nature of the Underworld was a small black dog, who came running up to the peak of a cliff.

Cerba.

"Hugo!" I screamed this time.

My heart did not slow down, and all of my cells came back to life, waving at his approach. A man dressed in elegance and power, wearing an inky black suit, came out of the shadows of the forest.

"We found him," I whispered.

The king of darkness looked heavenward to me, hands in his pockets as if he knew I'd come to his kingdom.

After all, once upon a time, I had inflicted chaos.

Sweet lily had become the bringer of death *that day.*

I did it all for Radcliff, and I'd do so. Much. More.

To everyone, I was a witch.

To him, a flower goddess.

But I was, too, the queen of hell.

To be continued…

Acknowledgements

Dear reader,

Thank you for being part of this journey and blessing me with your support. This is your sign to chase after your dreams and shine with your beautiful and unstoppable self.

From the bottom of my heart, I believe in you and wish you to attract all the happiness you deserve. Always remember not to be too hard on yourself, you're worthy. The world needs you, you have so much to offer. Never let the darkest of time tear off your light, and always have hope.

One word can change a life, just like your words changed mine. We may live on the opposite side of the world and be strangers, but to me, you're like a friend.

Remember that this is your story to write, and no one else but you can decide who you are and what you can achieve.

All the magical best,
From someone who never stops believing in her dreams.

Ps: Stay tuned for the release of the last book of the Scent trilogy.

CPSIA information can be obtained
at www.ICGtesting.com
Printed in the USA
BVHW040258140522
636990BV00002B/39